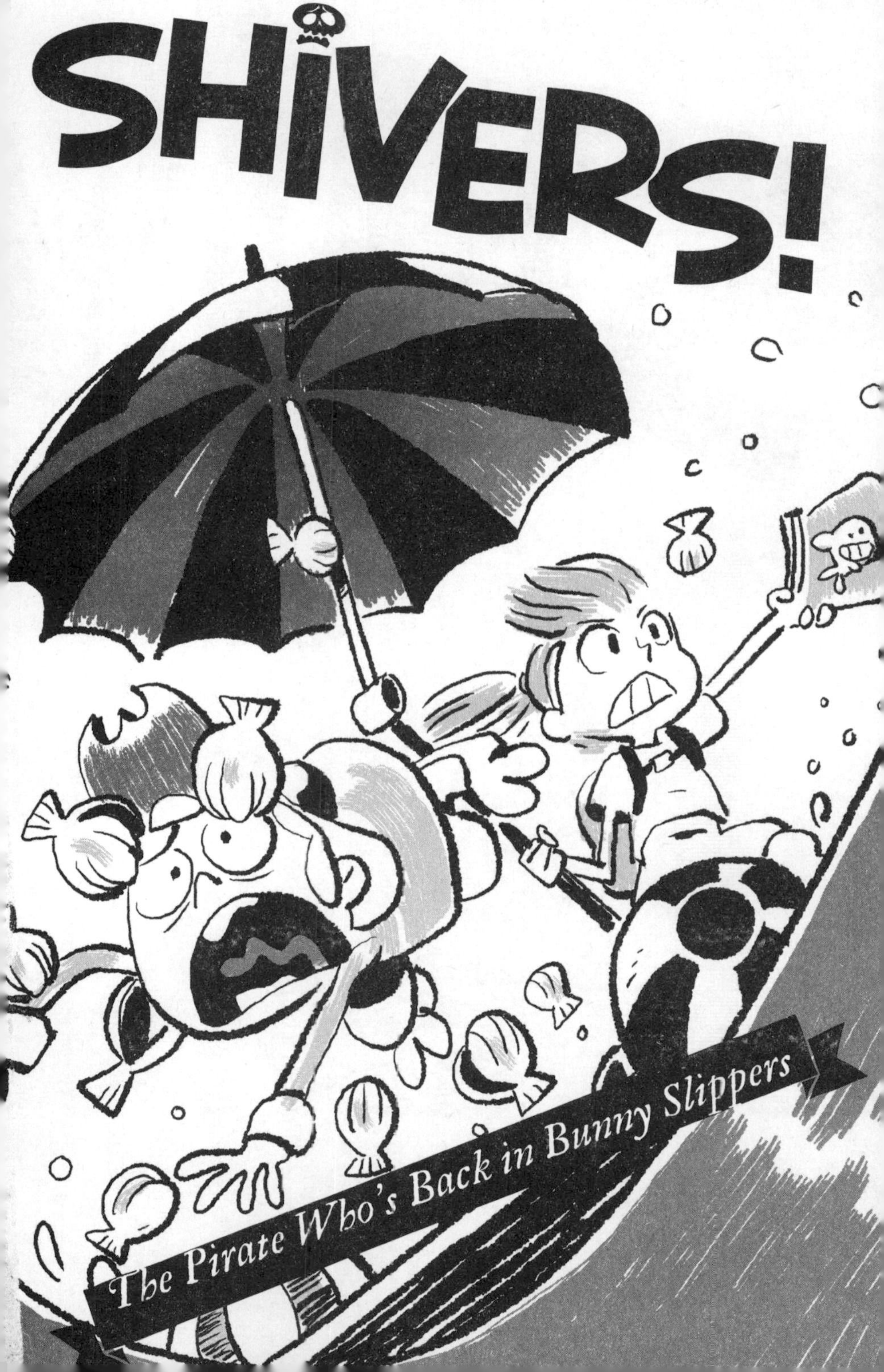
SHIVERS!
The Pirate Who's Back in Bunny Slippers

SHIV

BY ANNABETH BONDOR-STONE

AND CONNOR WHITE

ERS!

The Pirate Who's Back in Bunny Slippers

ILLUSTRATED BY
ANTHONY HOLDEN

BASED ON A REALLY FUNNY IDEA BY
HARRISON BLANZ, AGE 9

HARPER

An Imprint of HarperCollinsPublishers

Shivers!: The Pirate Who's Back in Bunny Slippers
Text copyright © 2016 by Annabeth Bondor-Stone and Connor White
Illustrations copyright © 2016 by Anthony Holden

Library of Congress Cataloging-in-Publication Data
Bondor-Stone, Annabeth, author.
    Shivers!: the pirate who's back in bunny slippers / by Annabeth Bondor-Stone and Connor White. –
First edition.
        pages   cm. – (Shivers! ; 2)
    "Based on a really funny idea by Harrison Blanz, Age 9."
    Summary: "Shivers, the pirate who's afraid of everything, is embarking on his second and scariest
adventure–this time to save his beloved ship, The Land Lady"– Provided by publisher.
    ISBN 978-0-06-231389-8 (hardcover)
    [1. Pirates–Fiction. 2. Fear–Fiction. 3. Adventure and adventurers–Fiction. 4. Humorous
stories.] I. White, Connor, author.   II. Holden, Anthony, illustrator.   III. Title.
PZ7.1.B665Sh 2016   2015009964
[Fic]–dc23   CIP
                                                                                                                AC

Typography by Joe Merkel
16 17 18 19 20 CG/RRDH 10 9 8 7 6 5 4 3 2 1
❖
First Edition

For Aisling and Nadine

CHAPTER ONE

TWO MINUTES.

The countdown had begun. One minute, fifty-nine seconds. One minute, fifty-eight seconds. Shivers the Pirate started to panic. Time was running out. He spotted an old pizza box on the counter. "Perfect!" he said, picking it up to use as a shield. *At a time like this,* he thought, *anything could come flying at my head.*

One minute, thirty seconds.

The sound was going to be ear-splitting— which was terrifying to Shivers. He already had two ears and he didn't need any more! He swiped two fluffy sponges from the sink and taped them

1

to his head to protect against the sound.

One minute.

He opened his cabinet and pulled out eight sacks of sugar and stacked them into a protective and delicious wall. He crouched behind the barrier, bracing himself for the worst.

Thirty seconds.

Something was missing! Shivers carefully peeked his head up and looked around the kitchen. Sitting on the table in his fishbowl was Shivers's first mate, Albee. Albee was happily munching away at his breakfast fish flakes, completely unaware of the chaos that was about to unfold.

Ten seconds.

"I'll save you, buddy!" Shivers cried, leaping out from behind the wall and running across the kitchen. He pulled Albee's bowl to his side, cradling it like a football. "Here it comes!" he shouted, diving behind the wall just as he heard the first BOOM! He held the pizza box over his head and did what he did best:

"AGGGGHHH!"

he screamed.

The explosions were in full force now. Shivers clutched Albee tightly. "We're going to make it through this," Shivers assured him. "And if things get out of hand, I have a backup plan." Shivers held up two garbage bags that they could use to parachute out the porthole.

The explosions were happening even faster now, and after each one, Shivers let out a little scream. So it sounded something like this:

POP!
"EEK!" POP! "YOW"
POP!
"BLAARG!"

Then, just when it seemed like the explosions couldn't get any louder, Shivers heard the sound he had been waiting for all along, the ring of sweet freedom that mean the battle was over: DING! He collapsed on the floor in a heap of sweaty relief. Finally, his breakfast was ready.

Shivers took the popcorn bag out of the microwave and settled in at the table, placing Albee on the chair next to him. "That was scary," Shivers said, tossing a kernel into his mouth. "But delicious. Want a piece?"

"Definitely not. Fish flakes for life!" said Albee.

But because he was underwater, and because he's a fish, it just came out looking like a few air bubbles. Shivers plopped a tiny piece of popcorn into Albee's bowl and it sank to the bottom.

Shivers smiled. His belly was full of popcorn. His trusted bunny slippers were on his feet. And most importantly, he was back safely at New Jersey Beach on his trusty pirate ship, the *Land Lady*. The *Land Lady* was a special pirate ship designed entirely by Shivers. It had more sunflowers than swords and more top hats than treasure. Instead of being stocked with cannons, it was filled with cans of peaches—which, he had determined through a series of tests, was the softest, friendliest fruit. But what really made the *Land Lady* special was the fact that it was planted safely in the middle of the beach and, if Shivers had anything to say about it, would never leave the land again. You see, his ship was almost lost on his last adventure. Which was also his first adventure. And, Shivers was hoping, his only adventure.

WHAM!

Shivers squealed as he heard someone kick open the front door of his ship.

Standing in the doorway with a wild look in her big green eyes was his best friend, Margo Clomps'n'Stomps. She was Shivers's best friend for three reasons. Number One: She helped him rescue his parents when they were trapped in the Statue of Liberty. Number Two: She was one of

the few people he wasn't terrified of talking to. And Number Three: She always brought snacks.

"Margo! I'm so glad you're here," Shivers said. "Did you bring snacks?"

Margo began, "Of course, but—"

"Great!" Shivers said, leading her into the kitchen. "We've got so much to do today! First, we have to organize my seashell collection from least to most threatening and get rid of the ones with sharp edges. Those things are really starting to freak me out."

"Shivers—" she tried to interrupt.

But Shivers inter-interrupted. "Then, it'll be time for a snack-nap, which either involves sleeping in the pantry or snacking in bed. I haven't decided yet."

"Shivers, listen—"

"And then, if we're feeling really bold, we can figure out which of my new rubber duckies would serve as the best flotation device in case of a bathtub flood."

Margo seized Shivers by the shoulders and shouted, "WE HAVE A PROBLEM!"

Shivers shivered. Problems were not his strength. Actually, they were. *Solutions* were not his strength.

Margo pulled a newspaper out of her big green backpack. She tossed the newspaper on the table and Shivers screamed. "AGGGH! Do we need to swat a fly?! Stay right where you are. I've got a pizza box that works great as a shield."

"No, Shivers," she said, holding up the front page of the paper. "Look!"

Shivers was shocked to see a picture of himself. For a moment, he thought his outstanding song and dance routines had finally made the news, but then he read the headline.

Shivers didn't understand why this was a problem. This picture showed him saving his parents and the rest of the pirates from the evil French chef Mustardio. Mustardio had trapped pirates inside the statue and forced them to make hot dogs—until Shivers came to the rescue.

Margo explained, "After we freed the pirates, the police came to find out what happened and they figured out that the Treasure Torch was gone."

"Not the Treasure Torch again!" Shivers groaned.

The Treasure Torch is the most valuable treasure in the Seven Seas, a majestic, towering flame made entirely of gold. No pirate has ever found it, but every pirate wants it—except for Shivers. It used to be at the top of the Statue of Liberty until Mustardio stole it and hid it somewhere. Shivers shuddered just thinking about it. "Every time that thing comes up, I end up covered in mustard and snails!"

"That was just one time," Margo corrected him. She flipped through the pages of the paper and continued, "Now, everyone is *really* mad. Especially Mayor President."

"Mayor who?!" Shivers asked.

But before Margo could answer, the ground beneath them lurched suddenly and they both tumbled to the floor.

"Did the ship just move?!" Margo asked.

Shivers gasped. "My *Land Lady*! She's trying to run away!"

Margo shot up and ran to the porthole to look outside. To her surprise, she saw a huge line of people dressed in black suits tugging ferociously on a rope that was tied to the bow of the ship.

Shivers grabbed Albee's bowl and held it up so they were face-to-fishy face. "It's the end of the world! Ships have grown legs!" he screamed. He poured Albee into a plastic baggie full of water so he would be ready to travel if they needed to escape. The ship lurched again and they all hit the deck. This time, before they could get up, the door flew open.

An enormous flood of people marched into the kitchen in a single-file line. Without saying a word, they lifted Shivers and Margo up above their heads.

"AGGGGHH!!" Shivers screamed, clutching Albee's bag.

"Put me down!" Margo shouted, wriggling like a worm on a waterbed.

The people in the black suits didn't listen. They carried them out onto the deck and chucked them overboard. As they flew through the air, Shivers wailed, "AGGH! Jagged rocks!" Actually, it was soft sand, and when they landed on it, it didn't feel too bad. But it didn't taste too good. Shivers spat out a healthy dose of mouth-mud and looked up, terrified of what he might see.

Standing in front of them was a woman in bright

purple pants and a matching suit jacket. She was wearing a pin with a picture of her own face on it. On the pin, she was smiling as brightly as a new lightbulb, but in real life, she was wearing a stormy scowl. She held a giant megaphone in one hand and she pointed it directly at Shivers as she spoke. "Shivers the Pirate! I am your mayor, Sheila B. President. But you can call me Mayor President."

Shivers winced. The sound was so loud that it rattled his rib bones and jellied his belly.

"During my time as your mayor, I have done some amazing things. Some might say super-amazing. Others might even say amazingly super. But this isn't about me. It's about you! The torch atop the Statue of Liberty has been taken! The very symbol of our national freedom—gone! I think we can all guess who is to blame. I'll give you a hint: YOU!"

"You didn't give us a chance to guess!" Shivers stammered.

"Shivers didn't steal the torch!" Margo added. Albee waved his fins in agreement.

"Oh, really?!" the mayor barked. "Then why is his picture on the front page of the newspaper? Why was he leading a mob of pirates out of the Statue of Liberty on the same day that the torch was found missing? I'll give you one guess. Because he stole it!"

"This is the worst guessing game ever," Shivers moaned.

"I know you have the torch, Shivers the Pirate!

And if you don't get it back to me by sundown tonight, I'm going to ban you from this beach forever!"

"Forever?!" Shivers, Margo, and Albee all shouted in a panic.

"What am I supposed to do?" Shivers asked. "Move the *Land Lady* out to sea?!"

"Wrong again!" The mayor grinned so her face matched the one on her pin. "If you don't give me back the torch, I'm using your precious ship for official government business." She pointed to some big buildings beyond the beach. "The New Jersey Elementary School basketball court needs a new floor. The Bank of New Jersey needs some new doors. And the New Jersey mayor needs a new wooden frame—for this picture!"

At that moment, out of nowhere, a photographer appeared and snapped a picture of the mayor standing triumphantly over Shivers's sand-caked face.

"Thank you, Roger," she said, patting the photographer lightly on the head. "This picture will be perfect for the front page of tomorrow's paper. I can see the headline now: 'Mayor Gets Torch Back from . . . Stupid . . . Pirate . . .' I don't know, I'm not a writer!" She pointed down at Shivers. "You have until sundown!" Then she snapped her fingers and shouted, "Interns!" The people in black suits rushed to her side, picked her up over their heads, and carried her to a long black stretch limousine that was parked at the edge of the beach.

By now, the rest of the interns had tied the *Land Lady* to the back of the limo. The limo sped away, dragging Shivers's home behind it.

He threw his sandy hands in the air and squealed in horror.

"It's going to be okay, Shivers," said Margo.

"Okay?!" Shivers wheezed. "Did you hear what she said?! I'm going to be banished! What am I going to do? Where am I going to live?! I'll be like a beaver without a dam . . . a bird without a nest . . . a snail without a shell . . ." Shivers's eyes widened in horror. "A slug!! I'm going to be a slug!!!!!"

Margo put her arm around him. "You're not going to be a slug. We're going to get the *Land Lady* back."

He stared out at the endless ocean. "How? It's impossible!"

"We'll find a way."

"Find a way? There's no way!" he said, shaking his head.

"Yes way! I know we can do this, Shivers. I know we can get the Treasure Torch."

Shivers gasped. "Are you crazy?! Our only hope is to get to my parents' ship so we can ask them to get the torch *for* us. It's all the way out THERE–"

"–and you know I get seasick!"

CHAPTER TWO

SHIVERS'S PARENTS WERE TWO of the most feared pirates on the Eastern Seas. If anyone had a chance of finding an unfind-able treasure, they could. They lived on a ship called the *Plunderer.* When they weren't sailing it on the high seas, they kept it anchored in the ocean, close enough to New Jersey Beach that they could see Shivers's night light every night. Still, it was too far for Shivers to get to, espe-cially without a ship.

"Why don't we swim?" Margo suggested.

"No, thank you! I already have a sinking feeling

in my stomach—I don't want a sinking feeling in my whole body!"

Margo took a second to scan the beach for a solution. "Then we'll need something that floats!" She grinned and sprinted away.

Shivers figured that Margo was talking about a root beer float, so he wandered toward the ice-cream shop while she scampered around the beach searching for supplies. By the time she got back, Shivers had had one midmorning snack and two panic attacks.

Margo unloaded her bounty onto the beach and quickly got to work.

"What are you doing?" Shivers asked. There was so much stuff, it made his head hurt. Actually, it was probably just the brain freeze from the root beer float. But he was still confused.

"I'm building us a world-class raft," she said as she tied two surfboards together. "This will be the base." Then she hoisted up a huge beach umbrella with rainbow stripes and wedged it between the boards. "And this will be our sail!" She grabbed an armful of bright orange floaties. "And these will be for–"

"ME!" Shivers snatched them from her and put two on each arm.

Margo sighed. Luckily, she had brought back-ups. She tied a bunch of beach balls together using the string from a kite, and strung them around the surfboards for extra floatation.

"It's unsinkable!" she declared. And no one who has said that about a ship has ever been wrong. "Plus, I brought a few beach towels in case we get wet. And some sunscreen–because that's just good sense."

"How did you manage to steal all this stuff without getting caught?" Shivers marveled.

"Shivers, I'm the daughter of a police officer. I would never steal! I just borrowed it."

Moments later, Shivers and Margo were on the raft. Shivers was holding Albee in one hand and his root beer float in the other. He was sitting with his legs crossed so his bunny slippers wouldn't get wet. Margo was in front of him, using the umbrella to steer the raft out toward the *Plunderer*. Suddenly, a wave rocked the raft and sent Shivers's ice-cream float flying into the ocean. It sank like a rock. "I've been lied to!" Shivers cried. Then another wave whipped them around, sending Shivers's stomach into a spiral of seasickness. He looked longingly back at his beach and thought, *If this plan doesn't work, I'm going to be stuck at sea forever! And there's nothing I hate more than–*

Shivers puked off the side of the raft.

"Gross!" Margo couldn't help but laugh. "At times like these you need to just close your eyes and imagine you're in the happiest place on earth."

Shivers closed his eyes and pictured himself

on a big stage, performing his most incredible song and dance time of all time. He kicked! He tapped! He shuffled! And just as he was launching into an amazing shake 'n' twist, he exclaimed, "Margo, it's working! I'm in my happy place! I can even hear the audience applauding!"

But really, Margo had accidentally steered the raft into a cluster of clams who *sounded* like they were clapping when they were *actually* clamping.

She tried to warn him. "Uh, Shivers—"

"Quiet, Margo! When the crowd loves you, you have to love them back." With his eyes still closed, he took a deep bow. His head hovered just above the water, so close that two clams snapped themselves right onto his eyebrows.

"AAAAAAGH!" he screamed, opening his eyes wide and whipping up so fast that he launched Albee's bag into the air. Margo let go of the umbrella to catch Albee, but that caused the raft to take a sharp turn. Shivers stumbled and toppled overboard. It was a clam calamity. They chomped onto his nose and clipped onto his lips.

"Hold still!" Margo cried, grabbing him by the shirt.

"They're trying to kiss me!!" Shivers called, wriggling around.

Margo mustered all of her strength and yanked him back onto the raft. His head was completely coated in clams, clicking and clacking their shells.

"You told me to go to my happy place, and now I'm stuck in this snappy place!" he screeched.

Margo tried to swat them away, but they were stuck on too tight. Then she got an idea. She grabbed the bottle of sunscreen and held it above Shivers's head. "Hope you're not trying to get tan,

clams!" she said, and then squeezed as hard as she could. The gloopy sunscreen poured down his head and carried the clams away on a slippery slide of SPF. They glided right off the raft and back into the water, sinking to the bottom of the sea right next to Shivers's root beer float.

"AAAAAAGH!" Shivers screamed.

"Why are you screaming?" Margo asked. "The clams are gone!"

"I know, but a teeny bit of that sunscreen got in my eye and it kind of stings."

Margo sighed. Sometimes with Shivers, you just couldn't win.

"I know that scream," bellowed a gruff but friendly voice. "Shivers!" It was his dad, Bob, peering over the deck of his ship. In all the clam commotion, they hadn't realized that they had drifted all the way to the *Plunderer.*

"What a surprise!" Bob grinned through his bristly beard.

Shivers's mom, Tilda the Tormentor, was next to

him. She was tall and strong, with wild, curly hair that always looked like it was trying to escape from the red bandanna wrapped around her head. "Tie up your . . . beach balls, and grab on to the anchor," she called down to them. "We'll pull you up!"

Margo pulled the beach towels from her big green backpack and knotted them end-to-end so they made a sturdy rope to secure the raft. Then she and Shivers grabbed on to the anchor. As Bob and Tilda pulled them up, Shivers clutched the anchor chain for dear life. "This is why I always make my parents visit *me*."

Finally, they reached the main deck. With Albee's bag in one hand, Margo hopped over the railing and onto the *Plunderer*. "Let's go, Shivers!" she called. "We don't have much time!" The sun hovered in the sky like a big, bright clock counting down the minutes until the mayor's deadline.

Shivers took a deep breath and grabbed on to the railing, then slowly rolled over until he plopped down onto the deck. It was not a pretty sight.

Bob pulled Shivers to his feet. Tilda hugged him so hard she nearly squeezed the popcorn right out of him. "Come on, your brother and your uncle are in the galley!" she said.

"Okay, but we can't stay and chat. We need you to find the—"

Bob swung open the door to the galley and a menacing cloud of black smoke billowed out.

"—FIRE!!!" Shivers screamed.

"You need me to find the fire?" Bob asked, confused.

"No, look!" Shivers pointed behind him. "Fire on the deck!"

There was a huge, blazing fire in the middle of the kitchen floor. Sitting beside it was Shivers's brave brother, Brock. Brock was bigger than anyone else in his family. He towered over Shivers and had so many muscles he almost looked lumpy. Next to Brock was Great Uncle Marvin, the crankiest pirate in the Eastern Seas.

"AGGHH!!" Shivers let out a scream that

turned into a cough. "Brock, do something!!"

"I am doing something. I'm making breakfast," said Brock.

"Haven't you ever heard of a microwave?!" Shivers shrieked in sheer panic.

"Haven't *you* ever heard of a breakfast fire?" Brock countered.

"NO!" Shivers dashed to the sink, filled a bucket with water, and threw it on the fire.

Uncle Marvin scowled and shook some water off his sleeve. "Now I've got a soggy sausage!"

Brock didn't seem to mind, though. He took

a bite and grinned. "Hey, not bad! It's soggy but scrumptious!" He crammed the rest of it in his mouth. "And I can eat it so much faster now!" Without a second thought, he stole Uncle Marvin's sausage off the stick and slurped it down.

Uncle Marvin stood up in a huff. "Why did I even bother putting my teeth in today?" He angrily stormed out of the room.

"Listen, everyone! There's no time for breakfast now!" Shivers said, horrified that he would ever have to utter those words. "Mom, Dad, you have to find the Treasure Torch."

Bob wiggled a fishbone toothpick between his front teeth and sent a piece of old meat flying across the room. "Son, we'd love to find the most coveted treasure in all the Eastern Seas but it's impossible!"

"Besides, we're already moving on to the next exciting treasure. The Long-Gone Jewels of Georgia!" said Tilda. Then she expertly hurled a dagger across the room toward a map on the wall. Shivers screamed as it whizzed past him and landed smack in the middle of the Georgia coast.

"No!" Bob shouted, pounding his fist on the table. "I want to capture the Crystal Canary of Canada!" He flung his own dagger like a Frisbee and it landed on the map above Tilda's. Shivers squealed and covered his face for protection.

Brock stabbed his dagger—which was actually a butcher knife—through the middle of the map, splitting it in two. "What about the famed Golden Arches?!" he cried.

"We keep telling you, we're not going to McDonald's!" Tilda sighed

"Excuse me," Shivers said, peeking out from behind his hands. "But I *really* need you to find the Treasure Torch for me."

Shivers told them about what had happened that morning. Or, at least, he tried to. But he got so caught up in how terrifying the whole thing was that he didn't even make it past the popping popcorn. Margo stepped in and explained that if they didn't find the Treasure Torch by sundown, Shivers would lose his ship forever.

Bob and Tilda looked at each other and smiled. "Shivers, you don't need your *Land Lady*," said Tilda.

"What?" Shivers balked.

"It's high time for you to hit the high seas," said Bob. "The *Land Lady* was great for a while, but we miss you on our adventures. Come live with us, and we'll sail the Seven Seas together—like a family should."

"Yeah, brother!" said Brock. "Even I'm living on board until dad finishes building my new ship!"

Brock's old ship, the *Brock 'n' Roll*, had been missing for days and by now he figured it had been eaten by a giant squid.

Shivers protested, "I can't live with you guys! Everything about your ship is terrifying!"

"What are you talking about?" Tilda asked.

"You almost burned the place down with a breakfast fire! I nearly lost a nose to your willy-nilly knife throwing! And you don't even have a microwave!"

"That's right! We have *huge* waves!" Bob said proudly.

Margo looked through the porthole. "And here comes one now!"

As a mighty wave rocked the ship, Bob, Brock, and Tilda all put their hands in the air like they were on a roller coaster. "WHEEEEEE!" they shouted.

"AAAAAGH!" screamed Shivers. He ran out of the room and Margo followed.

Just as he was slamming the door, Tilda called out, "Welcome to your new home!"

Shivers and Margo stumbled across the deck and grabbed the railing of the ship for balance. Shivers stared back at the shore, longing for the home he was sure to lose.

He whimpered, "I miss my *Land Lady*." It was something no one had ever said before. "There's no way I can live here. It's chaos!

That beach is where I belong. And"–his mind starting spinning like a squirrel on a Tilt-A-Whirl–"AGGGGHH!"

"What?!" Margo asked. "Do you see another clam?!"

"I just realized the most terrifying thing of all about losing my home."

"No more daisies? No more pillow forts? No more popcorn?" Margo guessed.

Shivers shook his head. "No more *you*."

Margo's face crumpled like a newspaper no one wanted to read anymore. Shivers was right–if he was off sailing the Seven Seas with his parents, they wouldn't be able to go on adventures together. As much as she wished she was a real pirate, she was just a normal fifth grader. And for some reason her teacher, Mrs. Beezle, did not allow absences for adventures.

"I can't lose you, Margo," said Shivers. "You're my best friend."

Albee gasped.

". . . Who isn't a fish."

Margo took off her sad face and put on her game face. She gripped the straps of her green backpack and said, "We'll just have to find the Treasure Torch and return it ourselves, then."

"But how?! Even my parents said it was impossible."

"Who cares what they said?" Margo said. "Bravery comes from within."

Shivers paused to think about that. "It does?"

"Yes," said Margo. "I read that in a fortune cookie once. Those things taste a lot like cardboard, but boy, do they give good advice."

Shivers took a deep breath, trying to muster all the bravery he could. There wasn't much there, but it was enough to make him say, "Let's go get it."

"That's the spirit!" Margo said. "Now, we just have to figure out where to start."

"I'll tell you where!" croaked Uncle Marvin. He was standing on the deck holding a jar labeled MARVIN'S LUNCH.

"AAAGH!" Shivers screamed. "How long have you been behind us?"

"The whole time! Where else am I supposed to pickle the raisins for my midday mush meal?" He started rifling through the pockets of his tattered coat. "AHA!" he cried, pulling a crumpled piece of paper out of his front pocket. He shoved it into Shivers's hands.

"Uncle Marvin, I don't want your old gum wrapper," Shivers grumbled.

"It's not a gum wrapper, you fuzz-brain!" Marvin spat. "It's instructions for how find that Treasure Torch."

Margo, Shivers, and Albee were blown away. And it wasn't even that windy out!

"How did you get this?" Margo said in awe.

"I stole it from Mustardio's office!"

Great Uncle Marvin had been trapped in Mustardio's hot dog factory for years. Usually, he was a regular at the onion-peeling station, but every once in a while Mustardio would make him clean his office floor with an old toothbrush—or, as Mustardio called it, a mini-mop.

"I was looking for some trash to spit my old gum into, and I found this. I thought it might be useful. Go on, open it."

Shivers uncrumpled the paper. Scribbled in black ink was the strangest letter he had ever seen.

Mustardio,

I followed your instructions, now you can ease your mind.
Your treasured torch is safe, I made it really hard to find.

I know that when the time is right you'll want to bring it home.
To get it back, just follow this mysterious, rhyming poem.

Chase your franks into the place where wieners pass the test.
Then look behind yourself to find the next step of your quest.

The festive stop where you must go will frankly seem quite strange.
For your next move, you must take note of how these Franks make change.

Don't overlook where Franks get francs to find your destination.
Now after all this rhyming I am going on vacation.

Fondly,
Francois

Shivers scratched his head. "How is this a clue? I don't even have a clue what he's talking about!"

"Who's this Francois guy anyway?" Margo asked, reading over Shivers's shoulder.

Marvin shrugged. "Some guy who almost got gum on his letter, that's who!"

Margo puzzled over the first line. "'Chase your franks into the place where wieners pass the test' . . . He must mean Mustardio's hot dogs."

"How are we supposed to chase hot dogs?" Shivers shuddered, imagining mutant hot dogs with tiny little legs running around.

Margo explained, "After Mustardio made the hot dogs in his factory, he must have sent them out to be sold. But where?"

Great Uncle Marvin piped up. "I'll tell you where! When Mustardio made me clean the packaging room, I looked at the labels on every box of franks. All of them were being shipped to a place called the Pig-Out Palace on Twenty-Fifth

Street in New York City. I'll bet my unbraided back hair that's exactly where you should go."

Margo and Shivers were pretty grossed out, but they were also very grateful.

Marvin hoisted himself up. "Now, leave me alone. I'm going to go sit in my bean bag."

"You have a beanbag chair?" Shivers asked.

"No, it's just a bag of beans I keep by my bed. The bean juice is good for my flaky skin," Marvin said.

"Ew . . ." said Shivers.

I wonder if that works, Albee thought, looking at his scales.

"Enough with the bean blabbing, we've got to get to the Pig-Out Palace!" cried Margo.

Shivers, Margo, and Albee got back on the anchor. As Marvin lowered them down to their raft, Shivers started to have second thoughts. "Are you sure there isn't *any* other way to save my home?" He put his head in his hands. This was bad.

"Come on, Shivers, it won't be that scary!" Margo said. "Maybe a few fistfights—"

"AGGGH!" screamed Shivers.

"A shipwreck or two–" she added.

"AGGGH!"

"And a few close brushes with death," said Albee, but luckily Shivers didn't hear him.

When they reached the water, they climbed onto the raft. Margo untied the towel rope and pointed the beach umbrella so they were on course for New York City. Shivers just stared up at the sky. It was high noon now and the sun didn't have anywhere to go but down.

CHAPTER THREE

BY THE TIME THE raft reached New York, Margo was exhausted. Every time Shivers got a little bit wet, she had to convince him that it was just salt water and not clam spit. Still, when they got to the shores of Manhattan she was thrilled. She couldn't wait to see what they would find at the Pig-Out Palace. "Let the adventure begin!" she cried.

"Aw, I was hoping we were already at the end," Shivers whined.

They ran past huge skyscrapers and honking taxis until they rounded a corner and saw a green sign telling them they had reached Twenty-Fifth

Street. The block was packed with more people than Shivers had ever seen. Funny-looking people, serious-looking people, and people who looked like they wanted to be serious, but were too funny-looking. There were people from all walks of life, all runs of life, and even one girl who seemed to be skipping through life.

"There it is!" Margo pointed to a flickering neon sign that said PIG-OUT PALACE in loopy writing beneath an enormous picture of a pig in

a chef's apron. "We have to go in there and find 'the place where wieners pass the test,'" she said, holding up the crumpled clue.

"What does that mean?" Shivers asked.

"Maybe the hot dogs have to pass a food inspection so the restaurant knows they're safe to eat."

Shivers gasped. "Or maybe Mustardio made a bunch of super-smart hot dogs and they all have to take a math test! And whichever one passes doesn't have to get eaten!"

Margo and Albee stared at him in wide-eyed silence.

"Or . . . the thing you said," Shivers said sheepishly.

Margo held up Albee's bag. "Albee, you supervise."

She opened the doors of the Pig-Out Palace, which were shaped like two giant hot dog buns. The doorknobs looked like two enormous dollops of ketchup. Shivers said nervously, "I hope this isn't the actual size of the food!"

But it was. There were no small portions at the Pig-Out Palace. The restaurant was packed with people carrying gigantic trays of food and each dish had an epic name that suggested maybe more than one person should be eating it. A man in a Hawaiian shirt was loosening his belt after finishing the Rib Rack Stack. A woman in stretchy pants and sports sandals was carrying a plate called the Insane Doggie Train, which was five hot dogs lined up end to end in one long hot dog bun. A little girl ordered a Milk Quake, which was a milk shake the size of a trash can. The man behind the counter made it for her by plopping a whole container of ice cream into a carton of milk and shaking it like a lunatic.

Shivers's mouth was watering but there was no time to eat. They scanned the dining room, but they didn't see anyone testing any hot dogs.

So they began to snoop around the rest of the 'rant. They checked out the coat check but all they found was a bunch of pocket lint and an old pack of gum. They snuck into the kitchen but only saw mixes and sauces and stews. By now, Shivers's stomach was growling so loudly, it sounded like he had eaten an Angry Bear—which was actually a dish on the menu here. If he didn't eat something soon, he was worried he wouldn't survive until snack time.

"Order up! One Meat Fleet!" said the cook, slapping down a tray with six huge slabs of meat on a bed of french fries.

"No one will miss one of these little guys," Shivers said. He handed Albee to Margo, hoisted himself up to the counter and snatched one of the fries. He popped it into his mouth and smiled, satisfied. But soon, the smile wrinkled into a queasy grimace. His face turned green like wilted lettuce. His stomach did somersaults, which really upset him since he had never taught his stomach gymnastics. He doubled over, moaning, then stumbled through the kitchen doors and into the dining room.

"What happened?" Margo wondered. "Uh-oh," she said, picking up one of the fries. "This isn't just a french fry. It's a curly fry! Shivers must be getting *C*-sick!"

Albee sighed. "Classic Shivers."

And with that, they heard a SPLAT! and then a collective "Ewwwwwww!" from the dining room.

"Let's hope that was just a Milk Quake spilling," said Margo.

Albee shook his head. It sounded like a Shivers Quake to him.

They ran into the dining room and found Shivers leaning over the salad bar, looking a lot emptier than he had before. Luckily, no one at the Pig-Out Palace ever ordered salad, so no one seemed to mind that Shivers had added a little more green to the mix.

"I guess I should have noticed that fry was

curly," Shivers said, wincing. Still a little queasy, he stumbled around and put his hand up to regain his balance. But what he thought was the wall was really a pair of double doors! When he leaned against them, they swung open and he toppled over onto the floor.

"Get away from there!" barked a man wearing a bright yellow T-shirt and a name tag that said, HELLO, MY NAME IS CARLOS, WELCOME TO THE PIG-OUT PALACE, HOME OF THE 25 FRANKS CHALLENGE. It was a lot to fit on one name tag.

Carlos yanked Shivers to his feet and pushed him aside. "You can't go into the Hall of Wieners!"

"The what?" Shivers asked.

Carlos snorted. "The Hall of Wieners! It's the place where we honor all the winners of the Twenty-Five Franks Challenge."

"The *what* what?"

"It's the most exciting competition you've ever seen in your life!" Carlos cried.

Shivers looked skeptical. "Clearly, you've never

been to the oven-cleaning competition at the New Jersey Mall. That thing really heats up."

"Okay"—Carlos rolled his eyes—"it's the second most exciting competition you've ever seen in your life. The contestants have to eat twenty-five hot dogs in two minutes. Whoever completes the challenge gets to enter the Hall of Wieners to receive a glorious prize!"

Margo gasped and pulled Shivers aside. "Do you know what this means?!" she said.

"Well, when someone says a prize is 'glorious,' it means that it's even better than fantastic—"

"No! Shivers, this is the place where wieners pass the test! And now we have to get inside. You have to win the Twenty-Five Franks Challenge."

"Me?! Win the challenge?" Shivers balked. "Why can't you do it?"

"I stayed up all night eating fortune cookies! No one ever told me that too much of a good thing becomes a bad thing! Well, that first cookie did, but I didn't listen."

Shivers looked at Albee with desperation in his eyes.

"Don't look at me, buddy," Albee said.

Margo urged, "Come on, Shivers. Aren't you hungry?"

Shivers was hungry. He had been hungry all day, and after the curly fry incident he'd lost his morning popcorn, his midnight salty snack, and last night's pancake dinner. So now he was hungrier than ever. But the idea of speed-eating in front of a screaming crowd gave him the heebie-jeebies.

Shivers turned back to Carlos and pleaded, "Isn't there any other way to get into the Hall of Wieners?"

"No! Wieners only. If you want to get in, you have to win." Carlos sneered. "So, do you think you have what it takes?"

Shivers didn't know what "it" was, but he was pretty sure he didn't. Before he could argue, Margo boldly said, "He's Shivers. I know he has what it takes!"

"Margo–"

"You can do it. I believe in you. Plus, your mouth is all stretched out from your constant screaming."

Carlos grinned and grabbed Shivers by his elbow. He pulled him across the crowded restaurant and up onto a stage, plopping him down behind a long table next to two other contestants. They both glared at Shivers.

Carlos picked up a microphone and his voice popped through the speakers. "Ladies and gentlemen, hold on to your buns! It's time for the Twenty-Five Franks Challenge!"

Everyone in the restaurant jumped up and started cheering wildly. As Shivers looked out at the raucous mob, he suddenly lost his appetite. It was horrible timing, too, because just then, Carlos pounded his fist on the table and screamed,

"BRING OUT THE FRANKS!"

CHAPTER FOUR

A BRIGADE OF WAITERS in bright yellow T-shirts and suspenders carried three gigantic buckets full of hot dogs up onto the stage. They plopped a bucket down in front of each contestant. By now, Shivers was really starting to panic. The lights were shining so brightly in his eyes that he could barely see. And the roar of the crowd was so loud that he could barely hear. He was hoping he could barely taste, too, because he was pretty sure he was going to be tired of hot dogs very soon.

The only upside to the whole thing was that Shivers got to wear a red-and-white-checkered plastic bib, which he thought looked very cool.

Carlos announced into the microphone, "As our returning guests already know, the rules are simple. Our contestants have two minutes—that's right, two minutes—to eat twenty-five pigtastic doggies. And if they succeed, they win fame, glory, and the surprise grand prize!"

Shivers gulped. He had heard about the prize, but no one had said anything about a *sur*prise.

Carlos continued, "Many have tried, few have won, and even fewer have made it through the night without ending up in the hospital. Let's meet our contestants!"

Carlos handed the microphone to the first contestant. He was a huge, muscular guy in a plaid shirt with the sleeves ripped off. He had a tattoo of a cheeseburger on his right arm. "I'm Jim," he said in a gruff voice that sounded like his throat was coated in cactus needles. "I'm a professional bowler, and I'm here to roll my competition straight into the gutter!"

The crowd went wild. A table full of Jim fans started hooting and hollering. One guy jumped onto his chair and crushed a root beer can on his forehead.

Jim passed the microphone to the next contestant, a tiny woman wearing a bright yellow dress with flowers on it. She had long brown hair tied in a ponytail and big red reading glasses hanging on a chain around her neck. "I'm Jackie. I'm a kindergarten teacher," she said in her softest inside voice. Then she cleared her throat and bellowed, "And I'm here to school everyone!!!"

The noise from the crowd got even louder. A class of kindergartners at the foot of the stage was shrieking for their teacher. They were holding signs above their heads that said GO MISS JACKIE! and MISS JACKIE WILL CRUSH YOUR BONES!

and LOOK HOW GOOD MY HANDWRITING IS!

Jackie passed the microphone to Shivers. "I'm Shivers," he said, his voice shaking. "I'm a pi–" He stopped himself, remembering that the last time he told a crowd he was a pirate, he got thrown off a boat.

"Pie . . . man." He stuttered. "And I'm here to . . . bake you into a pie."

The crowd suddenly went silent. A man in the back wearing a cowboy hat shook his head and said, "Not cool, man. Not cool."

Margo looked around nervously. She knew if Shivers was going to win this, he would need the crowd on his side. She had to act fast. She jumped onstage and grabbed the microphone. "What he meant to say was, he's the pie man, and he's ready for a slice . . . of VICTORY!"

The crowd went crazy again, shouting and stomping their feet.

"Don't worry, Shivers." Margo patted him on the shoulder. "I'm going to be your coach. And Albee's going to be your cheering section! Look, he's saying 'Woo!'"

"It always looks like he's saying 'Woo!'" Shivers grumbled.

"LET'S GET THIS PARTY STARTED!" Carlos shouted into the microphone, which made Shivers think Carlos didn't really understand why people use microphones. Then he held up a timer and announced, "Your two minutes starts . . . whoops! I hit the button on my stopwatch thirty seconds ago. You have ninety seconds. GO!"

A bell rang. The contest had begun.

As Jim and Jackie both dug in to the dogs, Shivers was so nervous he couldn't even decide which one to eat first. When he finally picked up his first hot dog, it slipped right out of his sweaty hands and plopped onto the table.

Meanwhile, Jim and Jackie finished their first dogs and a gigantic scoreboard lit up behind them with a loud DING!

It was the exact same DING! as Shivers's microwave back at home and it reminded him that if he couldn't finish these franks, and fast, he would be stuck at sea sucking down sliced swordfish for the rest of his life. Worst of all, he wouldn't even have Margo around to protect him if the sword-fish sliced back.

He looked down at his overheating hands. "Margo! My fingers are freaking out!"

"Just hold on tighter! You've got to get these doggies down!"

Shivers reached for another hot dog and gripped it as tightly as he could. Unfortunately, he gripped it so tightly that the hot dog became a shot dog and squeezed right out of the bun. The crowd gasped as they watched the weenie whirl through the air like it had sprouted wings. It landed right in the middle of someone's water glass with a PLOINK!

The bell struck again. "One minute left!" Carlos's voice thundered through the room. Shivers's score was still zero.

Margo dashed down from the stage and grabbed Shivers's soggy hot dog from the water glass. Then she ran back up and popped it in his mouth. He slurped it down in less than a second and then smiled, surprised. "Not bad!" he said. "It's like a long piece of Jell-O! Or really big spaghetti!"

"DING!" The scoreboard lit up behind Shivers and changed from zero to one. But Jim was on his seventh doggie and Jackie was already halfway through her tenth. They were like eating machines.

Margo thought back to when Shivers had dumped water on Brock's breakfast sausage and it had been much easier to scarf down. Her green

eyes lit up like two traffic lights that said "GO!" She held up the hot dog bucket. "Follow me. It's time to give these doggies a bath."

Margo ran back out into the crowd, gracefully tossing hot dogs from the bucket into any water glass she could see. She looked like the flower girl at the world's most disgusting wedding. Shivers was right at her heels, giving the doggies a second to soak, then scooping them up and gulping them down. The scoreboard behind him shot up to 7.

The crowd gasped. No one was expecting Shivers to catch up. But then they started shouting louder than ever.

"Ready for more?!" Margo asked.

"I sure am!" Shivers said as he drank a pitcherful of hot dogs in a single gulp. The scoreboard behind him now read 12, but Jim was at 17, and Jackie was already at 20.

"Ten seconds left!" Carlos shouted.

The crowd started counting down the final seconds.

Margo looked around in a panic. There were no more water glasses. She glanced at the water in Albee's bag.

"Don't even think about it," he said.

Just then, she was hit with an idea. Actually, it wasn't an idea. It was a splash from a fountain in the middle of the restaurant that was made of ketchup bottles squirting water in high arches. She spun around and held the bucket so the stream of water filled it up, drenching the dogs inside.

"Shivers! Flying hot dogs!" she shouted, and flung the contents of the bucket across the room. Shivers screamed as the hot dogs careened toward him.

He opened his mouth so wide that the hot dogs flew right in.

The final buzzer sounded as Shivers swallowed. His final score shot up to 25.

"We have a wiener!" Carlos announced into the microphone. There was a loud BOOM! and a glitter cannon shot sparkling confetti all over the restaurant. Everyone cheered, but the loudest cheer of all came from Margo. She was shouting and jumping up and down, which was not much fun for Albee.

Carlos put his hand on Shivers's shoulder. "Congratulations. I guess you do have what it takes. That enormous mouth of yours is a perfect doggie door!" He whisked Shivers through the cheering crowd with Margo following close behind. Shivers had never seen so many outstretched arms waiting to shake his hand. It was like being a rock star, or meeting a giant centipede.

Carlos marched them to the double doors that held their destiny. "Welcome to the Hall of Wieners," he said. He pushed open the doors, revealing a long corridor. The walls were lined with pictures in glimmering golden frames and a red carpet stretched all along the floor.

As Carlos walked them down the hallway, Margo whispered to Shivers, "We did it! We made it to the place where wieners pass the test." She pulled out the clue and examined it. "Now we have to 'look behind ourselves to find the next step of our quest,' whatever *that* means."

"Look behind myself . . . AAAGH!" he spun around. "Who's behind me? Is someone following me?!"

"No one is following you," Margo assured him. "Just stay sharp, okay?"

"That sounds awfully dangerous, but I'll try."

Shivers examined the pictures on the wall as Carlos continued the tour. There were dozens and dozens of them. "How come each winner is holding a different prize?" Shivers asked.

"Each contest has a grand prize that is donated by a different company," Carlos explained. He pointed to a picture of himself giving a snorkeling mask to a gangly girl in a polka-dotted dress.

"This contest was sponsored by Rose's Nose Hoses. It's a scuba shop down by the sea."

Carlos moved on to the next picture, in which he was handing a folding chair to a pimply guy in overalls. "This one was sponsored by Patty O'Furniture's Patio Furniture."

Then he gestured to the next picture. In this one, he was handing a big empty bag to a gruff guy in a leather jacket. "This one was sponsored by Matt's Rat Sacks."

"Yuck," Shivers recoiled. "What is that?"

Carlos chuckled and patted Shivers on the head. "Friend, if you live in New York City, you need to have a sack for your rats." He pulled Shivers over to a big, puffy armchair and sat him down.

Shivers sank into his throne and gazed at the

crowd gathered at the entrance to the hall, cheering and snapping his picture. *I guess this is the life of a wiener,* he thought.

"Now bring out the grand prize!" Carlos shouted.

A waiter rushed in carrying what looked like a golden cake box.

Carlos announced, "Our prize today was generously donated to us by local bakery Early to Bread, Early to Rise." He handed Shivers the box. "It's a fabulous pair of bunny slippers!"

Shivers looked down at the bunny slippers on his feet. "But I already have a pair!" he said, disappointed.

"Not bunny slippers. BUNny slippers! Fresh baked!" replied Carlos.

Shivers opened the box and saw that the slippers were made from two fluffy hot dog buns. "Thanks," he said through a grimace. "I'll keep them . . . forever."

"I wouldn't do that if I were you," Carlos warned. "Now, it's time for our picture!" He pulled a camera from his back pocket and handed it to Margo.

"Wait!" Shivers shouted. "This picture is going to be on the wall for the rest of time! And I'm still covered in hot dog water!"

"I think you look great," said Carlos. "But I also think yellow T-shirts and suspenders look great, so maybe I don't know what looking great looks like. Anyway, if you want to fix your hair there's a mirror over there."

Shivers went over to the mirror. It was in a gold frame engraved with the words "I'm a wiener, too!" Shivers liked that idea and thought if he ever got his *Land Lady* back, he would have to get a mirror just like it.

He started fixing his hair, adjusting his hat, and rebillowing his pantaloons. Margo walked up behind him and gasped when she saw his reflection. "Shivers!" she pointed at the mirror. "That's it! Look behind yourself!"

CHAPTER FIVE

SHIVERS STARED IN AN open-mouthed stupor, wondering if the next step of their journey could be behind his reflection in the mirror. It looked like he was doing an impression of Albee.

Margo couldn't wait any longer to find out. She grabbed the mirror frame and was about to push it aside when Carlos interrupted.

"Come on, let's take this picture! I'm on a tight schedule here. My life isn't all fun and games . . . it's mostly hot dog–eating contests!"

Margo knew she had to find a way to distract Carlos, if even for a few seconds. Then she was hit with a flash of genius. She looked at the camera Carlos had handed her and turned on the flash. She shoved Shivers back into the poufy armchair. Carlos stood behind him.

Margo held the camera up. "Say 'Cheese up to your knees!'"

"Hey, that's our most popular menu item!" said Carlos.

Margo pushed the camera in Carlos's face and snapped the picture. The flash went off, momentarily blinding Carlos.

"My eyes! My beautiful eyes!" Carlos wobbled around in a daze.

The picture wouldn't be great, but the result was exactly what Margo was hoping for. She sidestepped to the mirror and lifted it off the wall. Taped to the back was a faded, folded piece of paper. She peeled it off, stuck it in her backpack, and put the mirror back on the wall.

"Got it," Margo whispered to Shivers as Carlos finished blinking away the brightness.

They sped back to the entrance of the Hall of Wieners. Then they walked through the doors into the throng of Shivers's adoring fans. They twisted and turned, trying to make their way through the crowd and out of the restaurant. But at every twist and nearly every turn, there was someone trying to get Shivers's attention— waiters who wanted high fives, kindergartners who made him autograph their arms in crayon. Even the burly guy who'd crushed the root beer can on his forehead stopped to talk to Shivers, but he just wanted to know where the nearest hospital was.

They were finally about to reach the exit when the crowd started to shout, "Pie Man! Pie Man! Pie Man!" and they lifted Shivers up above their heads.

"I have to admit, being the King of the Wieners is pretty great!" Shivers called down to Margo. "I hope this feeling lasts forever!"

Just then Carlos's voice came over the speakers, "Ladies and gentlemen, welcome to the *next* Twenty-Five Franks Challenge!" Without hesitation, the crowd dropped Shivers on the ground and charged back to their seats to watch.

Shivers brushed himself off. "Wow. That was *exactly* fifteen minutes of fame. Well, I guess now all that's left for me to do is live a quiet life at home answering my fan mail."

"If we don't hurry up, you're not going to have a home to go back to," Margo reminded him. "Let's go!"

Outside the restaurant, the sun was blazing its way toward afternoon. The day was half gone and they had hardly cracked any of the clues. "At this rate," Shivers said, "we'll never find the Treasure Torch by sundown."

Margo and Shivers looked at the piece of paper that had been hidden behind the mirror. They realized the paper was a flier, and the cover showed a group of people holding hands in a circle. At the top of the page it said FRANK FEST in bright red letters.

"Frank Fest?" Shivers asked.

Margo shrugged and flipped through the brochure for more information. "It says here that it's the largest gathering of Franks in the entire world."

Shivers was more confused than a bear in a bookstore. "You mean it's a place where a bunch of people named Frank get together and hang out? That's the weirdest thing I've ever heard."

Margo pulled their original clue out of her backpack. "Well, Francois says right here that the 'festive stop where you must go will frankly seem quite strange.'"

"Well, I guess we have no choice," Shivers said with hot-dogged determination. "Let's find some Franks."

Frank Fest was located near the water's edge in the ballroom of the New York Hotel, which was famous for its fluffy feather beds, fabulous food, and gatherings of people with the same first name.

They ran to the hotel, past blocks and blocks of fancy shops, pet shops, and even a place where fancy pets could shop. Margo read the rest of the Frank Fest brochure while expertly swerving around bikers and businessmen. It's important to know that when she was in first grade, while all the other kids learned reading and writing, Margo taught herself reading and running.

"Frank Fest is a welcoming environment where we can all get together and Just Be Franks. Come meet some Franks and make some friends. But what are we telling you for? You already know all of this! Because your name is Frank! . . . It is, right? Because if it isn't, you really shouldn't be reading this and we will NOT let you in."

Margo stopped reading. Which also meant she stopped running. "Hm," she said. "We have a problem. The Frank Fest only lets in people who are named Frank."

Shivers was distraught. "What are we going to do? Find someone named Frank to help us? But I don't have any friends named Frank! Unless–" He looked at Margo and Albee. "Are you guys named Frank? No, of course not! Do I have to change my name to Frank? I can't do that! My name is who I am! I'm Shivers the Pie Man!"

Margo would have pulled her hair out in frustration if she had been listening. But instead, she was scribbling a solution. She taped a piece of paper on her shirt, another on Shivers's shirt, and one on Albee's bag. Albee wasn't wearing a shirt. Shivers looked down and read aloud, "knarF si eman ym ,iH." He scratched his head. "Margo, are you left-handed?"

"Yes, I'm left-handed but I know how to write. You're reading it upside down," she explained. "Here, read mine."

"Hi, my name is Frank," he recited. "Oh . . . trickery?" His voice started to quiver. Tricks made him uncomfortable. He had heard they were for kids, but they seemed very adult. "Do you think it'll work?"

"Only one way to find out," she said, and they ran the rest of the way to the New York Hotel.

As they walked into the lobby, Albee noticed a sign that said NO SHIRT, NO SHOES, NO SERVICE. He crossed his fins that no one would notice him.

In the corner of the lobby was an entrance to a grand ballroom with a huge banner above it that read FRANK FEST! JUST BE FRANK! There was a long line of people all waiting anxiously to get inside.

The wait felt long to Shivers, but even longer to Margo and Albee since they had to spend most of the time listening to Shivers go on about what he called The Dangers of Lines. Those dangers included: there's always someone sneaking up behind you; what if it's really a circle that goes on forever; and if one person falls, everyone else will fall like a bunch of dominoes.

When they finally reached the entrance to the ballroom, two men seated behind a table greeted them. One was wearing a golf shirt and a visor

shadowing his freckle-flecked face, and the other
was wearing a fancy suit.

"I'm Frank,"
said Fancy Frank.

"So am I!" said Freckles. "You must be Frank,
Frank, and Fish Frank."

"That's right!" said Margo.

"Welcome to Frank Fest!" said the Franks at
the same time.

"Frank you!" Shivers said.

Fancy and Freckles burst out laughing and

patted Shivers on the back. He was about to walk into the grand ballroom, when Freckles Frank stopped him. "Say, are you sure your name is Frank?" he asked.

Beads of sweat started to form on Shivers's head. This was why he hated tricks. He was so terrified that he forgot how to speak. And now he couldn't even remember what question the Franks asked him, let alone what the right answer was.

"Hey, buddy, I'm just franking your chain!" Freckles said. "Of course you're a Frank, you've got that awesome name tag!"

"Don't forget your welcome gift!" Fancy Frank said, holding out a yo-yo with an *F* on both sides.

"No way!" Shivers recoiled. "When I drop something on the ground, I prefer that it stays down there, not come spinning back up at me like it wants revenge."

Freckles and Fancy eyed each other, confused. Margo said, "I'll take one." It seemed like an odd gift, but then again, these Franks threw an odd fest.

She threw the yo-yo in her backpack as she made her way past the table and into the ballroom.

Inside, it was so crowded it looked like there was a sea of Franks surging throughout the room. The roar of their chatter was almost as loud as waves in a storm. The Franks were as different as could be–men, women, and kids of all shapes and sizes. They had names like Francis, Franklin, Frankfurt, Francesca, and there was even one guy named Frankenstein. But at the fest, everyone was just Frank.

They wove their way through the crowd but didn't make it far before a tall Frank tapped Shivers on the shoulder and pointed at Albee. "Is he here for the Frank Tank?" Behind him was a huge fish tank with all kinds of fish swimming around inside. "We like to give our Fish Franks the opportunity to get to know each other. You know, swim, blow bubbles, eat Frank flakes," the tall man exclaimed proudly. "I'm sure your fish would love it in there!"

"Albee?" Shivers asked.

Margo stared daggers at Shivers, which he thought was extremely unsafe.

"Ahem." Shivers cleared his throat. "*I'll be* happy to hand over my fish. My fish who is definitely named Frank!"

"Well, of course he is," the tall Frank said. "Look at that awesome name tag!" He took Albee from Shivers's hands and poured him from his bag into the tank.

Albee plunged into the new water and found

himself facing a shimmering pink guppy with a
bright yellow tail.

The charade begins, he thought. Then he said,
"I'm Frank."

"Aren't we all?" the guppy replied.

Albee chuckled at her sparkling wit. Before he
knew it, they were discussing art and science and
the meaning of life, and eating more Frank flakes
than he ever thought possible.

Margo and Shivers carved their way through
the enormous ballroom and got a better look at
how much the Frank Fest had to offer. There
was a sign that said FRANK FEELINGS CIRCLE, and
underneath was a group of Franks sitting on

pillows, crying and hugging. Nearby, there was a fenced off area called FRANK'S KITTY CORNER, where a gray-haired lady in overalls and fluffy socks corralled a bunch of mewing kittens and cooed, "Here, Frankie Frankie Frankie." There was a tent labeled FRANK'S FASHIONS. Franks would go inside and after a few minutes, come back out wearing a matching shirt, socks, and shoes, looking frankly fabulous. "I wonder if they have any bibs in there?" Shivers asked. "I've really been getting into those lately."

But Margo was too busy for bibs. She was puzzling over the next part of the clue: "You must take note of how these Franks make change."

"Change what?" Shivers wondered aloud. "Change the channel? Change a light bulb? Change their minds?"

They looked all around but there was no sign of a solution. There was, however, a sign of a sign. It was a big sign just above a red velvet tent. It said FRANK'S TREASURE TROVE in letters that seemed to float like smoke out of a genie lamp.

But what really grabbed Shivers's attention was a magnificent piano at the tent's entrance. The piano was black and white and perfectly polished so it shimmered in the light. Its gleaming white keys stretched out like a big toothy smile. And Shivers smiled back. And the best part was the piano was playing a song all by itself.

His eyes bulged like baking biscuits and he said, "Maybe the clue means change . . . their tune!!!"

"I don't think–"

But before Margo could respond, Shivers had tap danced over to the tent and gone inside. She had no choice but to follow him in.

The Treasure Trove was an antique shop filled from floor to ceiling with the oddest, oldest objects Shivers had ever seen. There was an entire wall covered in clocks all set to different times, shelves packed with a variety of globes— both regular and snow—and at least six suits of knights' armor. There were dozens of paintings

of old boats and big dogs and even a framed picture of a soup can with price tag that said, IF YOU
HAVE TO ASK, YOU CAN'T AFFORD IT.

It was all so overwhelming to Shivers that he
thought he felt a scream coming on, but it turned
out to be a sneeze. The place was really dusty.

"Hello?" Shivers called out, wondering if there
was anyone in there.

"Welcome to the Treasure Trove," a man replied,
popping up from behind the counter. He had a
low, gravelly voice and an accent that sounded

like he had peanut butter stuck to the roof of his mouth. It made him sound extra mysterious. He had crooked eyes, and three silver teeth jutting through a crooked smile. A thin gray mustache drooped over the corners of his mouth and down past his chin. "You must be Frank and Frank."

Shivers figured this man must be named Frank, too. He put his arm up on the counter and said, "I saw that fantastic piano out front and I just had to see what was inside your shop!"

"Oh, it's not much," Frank said bashfully. "Just a small part of my collection of the finest, rarest oddities from around the world. So, you're interested in the porcelain panda piano from Paris?"

"*Very*," said Shivers. "I've always wanted a self-playing piano."

"Actually, it's being played by a ghost."

"AAAAAAAAAGH!" Shivers screamed.

"I'm just kidding," Frank chuckled. "But it is extraordinarily expensive. You have such a lovely screaming voice. Do you sing?"

"Do I sing?!" Shivers shouted. "Is the ocean filled with giant squids?"

Frank shrugged. "Uh, I don't—"

"YES! Yes to everything!" Shivers said.

"Well then, you might be interested in this!" Frank held out a beautiful blue velvet top hat dotted with shimmering sequins that sparkled like stars in the night sky. "It's a topaz top hat from Tokyo."

"I love it!!!!!!" Shivers shouted, snatching the hat and shoving it onto his head. "I'll take one. No, forget it. I'll take a thousand!! No, that's too many. I'll take a hundred!"

"That'll be five hundred francs."

"What?" Shivers was perplexed. "But I'm only one Frank."

"Not Franks, francs! The coins they used to

use for money in France. It's the only accepted currency here at Frank Fest."

"Francs?! I've never heard of those before in my life! Are you sure that's a real thing?"

"It's as real as me," Frank said, holding up a silver coin. "This is a French franc, and I'm a French Frank."

"Ohh, so that's why it sounds like your mouth is stuffed with peanut butter," Shivers said.

Frank laughed and handed Shivers the coin. "If you want a hundred of those hats, you're going to need a big chunk of change."

"Change!" Margo and Shivers shouted at the same time.

Margo looked at Frank apologetically. "Will you excuse us for a second?" Then she took the top hat off of Shivers's head and held it to the side, hiding their faces so they could have a private top hat chat.

"So now we know how the Franks make change," Margo whispered.

"Francs!!!" Shivers cheered.

Margo took a closer look at the silver coin and noticed the strange spelling of "franc." She took out the clue and examined it. "It's even spelled the same in the next part of the clue: 'Don't overlook where Franks get francs to find your destination.'"

"So where do these Franks get their francs?"

"It must be where everyone gets money—the bank!" Margo grinned.

"You mean we're going to find our destination?! We're going to get the Treasure Torch?!" Shivers beamed.

Margo nodded and they jumped up and down excitedly. Then Shivers lowered the top hat and they saw that Frank was looking at them strangely, his crooked eyes even more crooked than before.

"This hat smells a little weird. I'll have to think about it!" Shivers tossed the hat back to Frank, and he and Margo darted out of the store.

Back in the bright lights of the ballroom, Margo knew exactly where to go. She led Shivers across the room to a brightly lit sign that said FRANK BANK. The Frank Bank was a big metal machine bolted to the wall. It looked just like a token machine at an arcade, except instead of giving out useless tokens

FRANK BANK

"MAKE
A
CHANGE
HERE
&
NOW"™

it gave out useless foreign currency.

Margo stared at the clue, reading out loud: "Don't overlook where Franks get francs to find your destination." She balled her fists up impatiently. "We're not overlooking it! We're looking right at it!"

Shivers shrugged. "Maybe we're overthinking it, and we just need to underlook it."

"What does underlook mean?"

"It's what I do to my bed before I go to sleep to make sure there aren't any monsters under it." And with that, Shivers crouched down, covered his eyes with one hand and reached under the machine with the other. "Dust bunny . . . Dust bunny . . ." And then, "NOT DUST BUNNY!" His hand flew back like a turtle on a treadmill. "Margo, there's something under there. It may or may not be a monster. Your turn to check."

Margo sighed and got down on the floor. She felt around to see what she could find. Suddenly, her hand brushed against something cold. She wrapped her fingers around it and pulled out . . .

"A key!" she exclaimed. In her hand was a big silver key. Engraved on the side were the words BANK OF NEW JERSEY: VAULT 25.

"Bank of New Jersey? That's right by my beach! It's been there the whole time? I knew those clams were trying to send me back to shore!"

Shivers's heart was pounding like the bass drum in a marching band. They had found their destination. All they had to do was open this vault and then he could get the Treasure Torch and return it to the mayor. And then he wouldn't have to lose his beach, or his ship, or his best friend.

"We solved the clue! We solved the clue!" Margo cheered, jumping up and down and waving the piece of paper above her head triumphantly. "Take that, Francois! Whoever you are!"

Suddenly, the clue was plucked from her fingers and they heard a peanut-buttery voice say, "Whoever *I* am?!!!!!!"

CHAPTER SIX

MARGO AND SHIVERS GASPED for air, but all they got was a mouthful of scare. Standing above them was the man from the Treasure Trove.

"*You're* Francois?" Margo stuttered.

"I thought your name was Frank!" Shivers stammered.

"Francois is French for Frank!" Francois barked.

Shivers couldn't believe it. "But if you're Francois, that means you–"

"Wrote this clue! Yes!"

"But *that* means you–"

"Hid Mustardio's torch for him! Yes!"

"And *that* means you're—"

"Really good at finishing sentences! I know!"

"Why would Mustardio trust you to hide his torch?" Margo said suspiciously.

Francois arched his crooked eyebrows. "Because that's what brothers do."

"That evil hot dog bully was your brother?!" Shivers squeaked.

"Yes. And everyone always said he was the *nice* one in the family." Francois lunged at Margo and roared, "Now give me that key!" He tried to grab her but she darted away just in time. Instead, he caught Shivers's shirt and pulled, ripping his name tag right off. Francois gasped. "Your name isn't even Frank, is it?!"

"Uh, not exactly . . ." Shivers squirmed. "It's Shivers."

"SHIVERS!" Francois screamed. "You're the pirate who blew up my brother!"

Shivers looked at Margo in desperation. She looked back with determination and yelled,

"RUN!"

They tore off toward the exit. As they ran, Shivers looked down at his empty hands and realized something was missing. "My first mate!" he screamed,

and he made a hard right toward the Frank Tank. It was a really hard right because he smashed straight into a wall. But he picked himself up and got back on track. They found Albee still deep in conversation with the guppy. Margo handed Shivers a spare sandwich bag from her backpack. He plunged the bag into the tank and scooped Albee up without anyone seeing.

"Can't you see we're in the middle of something!?" Albee shouted.

But his voice was drowned out by an announcement echoing through the ballroom. Francois's voice crackled over the speakers. "Attention, Franks. There are two traitors among us. Do not make friends with them, they are frauds! One is wearing billowy pantaloons and the other has a big green backpack and a stolen silver key. Do NOT let them get away!"

Gasps of shock and surprise rippled through the ballroom. Every Frank in the Fest looked around suspiciously, then their gazes zeroed in on Shivers and Margo. They started running toward them, yelling angrily and shaking their fists.

Margo began backing away slowly. "We have to think fast."

"No!" Shivers declared. "We have to run fast!"

They scrambled around the Frank Tank and away from the mob, but the fury of Franks followed close behind. They looped around Frank's Flank Steaks, which smelled delicious, and whizzed past Frank's Stinky Sneaker Supply, which smelled awful. Soon they were at the Frank Feelings Circle. Margo stopped short like a baseball player on opposite day. She grabbed two fluffy red pillows from the ground and planted her feet. "PILLOW FIGHT!!!!!!"

The Franks ran at her, and one by one she batted them away until their faces were filled with more feather and fluff than a duck in the dryer. She swung one pillow above her head like a lasso, then flung it through the air, knocking out a whole line of Franks. She put another pillow on her head like a football helmet. "This one's called the pillow plow!" she announced, then ran head-first into all the Franks she could find. "Come on, Shivers, get in here!" she shouted.

But Shivers was too busy testing the fluffiness of each pillow. He loved pillows but hated pillow fights. *Why ruin a good thing?* he thought.

Margo was down to her last pillows and the flood of Franks wasn't stopping anytime soon. They had to retreat.

They ran as fast as they could. Albee bounced in his bag like a bingo ball. With the stampede of Franks on their heels, Margo and Shivers ducked into Phrank's Photo Booth and, just as quickly, snuck out the other side.

"Get them!" one Frank cried.

"Where are they?!" another Frank asked frantically.

"Over by you, Frank!" a Frank responded.

"Who Frank? Me Frank?" asked Frank.

"No, not you, Frank, the other Frank!" Frank answered firmly.

"I'm Frank!" said fifteen other Franks.

All the confusion bought Shivers, Margo, and Albee some extra time. "Over there!" Shivers yelled, pointing to the exit. But he was screaming so much it sounded more like "AAGGHVER THAAAAGHR!!"

He led Margo around a corner and down a long, narrow row of Frank shops. Then he led her around another corner. But the faster they ran, the closer the sound of the mob became.

"They're catching up!" Margo yelled.

Shivers took her around one more corner and they skidded to a halt. They were right back at the photo booth where they'd started. Margo and Albee scowled at Shivers.

"Sorry! Sorry!" Shivers fretted. "I forgot that three rights make a wrong."

Margo panicked. "What are we going to do?"

Shivers looked around and saw that straight ahead was the Frank's Fashions tent. "I know what we have to do," he said, balling up his fists. "We have to go shopping."

"Shivers, forget about the top hat!" Margo urged.

"Trust me." Shivers ran at full speed toward Frank's Fashions and as soon as he reached the tent, he yanked Margo inside.

He whirled around the tent in a fashion frenzy, grabbing clothes off the shelves. He covered up his pantaloons with a pair of purple pajama pants and tied a big orange belt around his waist. "There's no time to color-coordinate!" he said frantically. Then he put Margo's big green backpack into a bigger blue backpack and placed a floppy yellow hat on her head, tucking her ponytail underneath it. Finally, he tied a cape around each of their necks. He stood with Margo in front of a full-length mirror, took one look, then snapped his fingers and said, "Make it work!" He grabbed the franc from his pocket and dropped it on the counter next to the cash register. "I hope this covers it."

"I hope this covers *me*," said Margo, pulling the cape up in front of her face like a vampire.

They all took a deep breath and walked back out into the ballroom. The Franks were getting frantic. They were looking everywhere—peeking under the carpets at Frank's Flooring, digging in the dirt at Frank's Ferns, even checking under the chickens at Frank's Feathered Friends.

"Maybe they never existed in the first place!" shouted the frustrated man who ran Frank's Fables.

Shivers, Margo, and Albee made their way across the room toward the exit without anyone giving them a second glance. "It's working!" Margo said in a hushed voice.

"HEY!" one Frank yelled, pointing at them. They froze in terror. "Great outfits!" the Frank said, smiling approvingly.

"This is the best plan I've ever had," said Shivers.

They had almost reached the doors that led out of the ballroom when the guy from the Frank Tank stepped right in front of them. "Hey, little Frank. How did you get out?"

Just then, Francois made another announcement

that boomed through the room: "Traitor update! They are NOT under the chickens! Stop looking under the chickens! Also, they have stolen a fish who is definitely named Frank."

The tall Frank's face turned so purple with anger that he looked like Shivers's pajama pants. "TRAITORS!" he cried, and grabbed Albee's bag.

"Let go!" Shivers bellowed, but Frank held on tight and screamed, "I'll save you, little Frank!"

The bag stretched and Shivers shrieked, but Albee had learned a thing or two from Margo's Pillow Plow and he knew exactly what to do. He swam at Frank's hand with all his might, crashing into it with his head. And if you think about it, fish are just big floating heads with teeny tails.

"My. Name. Is. Albee!" Albee said in a voice so magnificently menacing it was really too bad that no one could hear it.

His fish force sent Frank's hand flying off the bag.

They ducked between his legs, and Margo kicked open the doors. She led Shivers and Albee into the sunlight and down the street. The Franks were left in their dust, angrily shaking their Frank fists.

"We have to make a beeline for the raft," Margo called to Shivers as they ran.

"It had better be a really fast bee."

Soon, the afternoon would melt into evening, and Shivers was getting nervous. If he didn't get the Treasure Torch back to Mayor President by the time the sun set, he would have to brace himself for a life filled with nothing but watery terror. He thought about what living on the *Plunderer* would be like, and it was not a pretty picture. It was more like a scary movie. There'd be no Margo—and no microwave!

Margo could see that Shivers was concerned. He was pretty bad at hiding his emotions—in fact, he had been screaming his head off for the last

five minutes as they sprinted through the city. They finally reached the water's edge where the raft was docked.

"Shivers!" Margo shook his shoulders and he stopped screaming.

"Sorry, I was deep in thought. Sometimes I need time for quiet contemplation."

Margo sighed and they hopped on the raft. They set sail–or, rather, set umbrella–for the Bank of New Jersey. All they had to do to get there was cross the New Jersey River. At least, that's what the New Yorkers liked to call it. The New Jersians liked to call it the New York River. That way, neither of them felt responsible for cleaning up the garbage.

"This river is filthy!" said Shivers. "Are we sailing through bathwater?"

Shivers was afraid of baths so on the rare occasion that he took one, things got pretty grimy.

As they sloshed through the water, murky river sludge began to creep up onto the raft. Brown algae stuck to the bottom of the beach balls and ship scum sloshed up through the space between the surfboards. The rope tying the boards together became covered in seaweed. Actually, it was riverweed, which is seaweed covered in trash. The rope was so wrapped up that it turned completely green. It looked a lot like a slimy—

"SNAKE!!" Shivers shrieked. He threw his arms up and spun around in a circle. "Get it off! Get it off!"

"Shivers, it's just . . ." Margo tried to explain but he was in no state to listen. (Actually he wasn't in any state at all, he was between New York and New Jersey.)

He kicked at the rope but that just caused it to

wrap around his bunny slipper. "It's got a taste for rabbit!!" he screamed. Then he flung his foot up like he was punting a football. The rope unraveled and went soaring through the air.

For once, it was Margo who was frozen in terror. They really needed that rope.

Shivers breathed a sigh of relief and smiled at her. "Just doing what I do best. Keeping us safe."

And with that, the raft split in half. The surfboards were swept up in a swirl of raging river. The floaties became flotsam. The beach balls bounced above as the current slurped up Shivers, Margo, and Albee like they were the last drops of a Milk Quake.

CHAPTER SEVEN

MARGO SWAM BACK UP to the surface and gasped for air. She spotted the beach balls from the raft bobbing close by, still tied together by the kite string. She paddled over to them, fighting the current with all her strength. Shivers was nothing but a screaming head in the water. He couldn't swim, but he could kick and flail. Albee's bag of water was underwater, but he didn't seem to mind. Margo dragged the chain of beach balls toward Shivers until it was within reach of his flapping hands.

"Get on!" she shouted, then got hit with a mouthful of river water.

He gripped on to the first beach ball and it rolled forward so he was floating on top of it. Margo scooped up Albee and latched on to the beach ball in the back. It looked like they were riding a train of beach balls. Shivers was the conductor and Margo was the caboose. By the sound of it, Shivers was also the train whistle.

Margo tried to steer them back on course, but her paddling was no match for the current. They were being whisked down the river and out to the gaping mouth of the Eastern Seas.

"Not the open ocean!" Shivers shouted. "We're gonna be fish food!!!"

A fisherman standing on a bridge above the river smiled eagerly. "Did somebody say fish?" He pulled back his fishing pole and cast his line into the water.

The current pulled Shivers and Margo under the bridge and the fishhook caught onto Shivers's beach ball. There was a thunderous POP! as the ball exploded, flinging Shivers into the water. He dragged himself up onto the next beach ball in the chain.

They drifted closer and closer to the ocean, and the water was getting rougher. "INCOMING!" Margo pointed to a floating hunk of junk that was just a few feet away. It looked like an island of crushed light bulbs and shattered bottles, with jagged edges sticking out in all directions. Shivers closed his eyes and braced himself. As they whizzed past the trash, Shivers's beach ball bumped into the sharp end of a broken golf club and popped. He screamed and scrambled up onto the only beach ball left—Margo's.

Shivers held on to the ball while Margo clutched Shivers's shoulders. They see-sawed back and forth as the ball tossed and turned amid the trash. Shivers almost got a mouthful of old mousetraps. Margo narrowly missed a noseful of moldy eggshells. Then, for a moment they were both balanced perfectly. "Hold on tight!!" Margo commanded. Shivers was so gripped with fear that holding on tight wasn't a problem. In fact, he was too good at it. He squeezed so hard the ball popped into a hundred pieces.

Shivers, Margo, and Albee hit the water with a splash. They searched around frantically for something to grab on to. Finally, Margo spotted the beach umbrella that had been on the raft. She kicked her way over, pulling Albee along with her. She clutched the umbrella's handle just as a huge gust of wind blew by, opening it up. "We've got our sail back!" she said triumphantly. Shivers managed to hold on to her ankle just before another gust of wind sent them skidding out into the sea.

"Where are we going?!" Shivers wailed.

"There!" Margo pointed to a towering black ship not far in the distance. The hull was lined in metal spikes. The flag was black and red, with a picture of a flexing arm with muscles made out of boulders.

"There?! No way!"

"We have to get out of this water somehow!" Margo steered the umbrella so they were propelled toward the ship.

"But we don't know what kind of pirate is on there! Look at his ship! He's probably a crazy person! He's probably a maniac! He's probably–"

They reached the ship and someone poked his head over and peered down at them.

"Hey, brother!"

"Brock?!" Shivers and Margo were stunned. Albee wasn't fazed.

Brock threw them a rope and pulled them on board. "Dad just finished building my new ship! What do you think?"

"It's terrifying!" Shivers replied.

"Aw." Brock smiled. "You're just saying that to make me feel good."

"Does it have a name?" Margo asked.

"*Solid as a Brock*! Because nothing can break it!" Brock punched the deck as hard as he could. "See, that actually really hurt," he said, rubbing his knuckles. "So what were you guys doing in the middle of the river? Did you need a place to throw out your extra trash?"

Shivers and Margo told Brock all about their journey and explained that they needed to get to the Bank of New Jersey, find the Treasure Torch, and return it to the mayor, all before sundown. They had to move fast. It was almost dinnertime.

Brock was impressed. Then he was horrified.

"Let me get this straight. You're one step away from finding the most valuable treasure in the Eastern Seas. And then you're going to *return* it?!"

Shivers nodded sheepishly.

Brock put his head in his hands. "Classic Shivers." Then he set the course for the shores of New Jersey and the bank.

As they sailed, there was enough time for Brock to give them a tour of his new ship. He showed them the Wall of Knives. A warning sign was posted on the wall that said, CAREFUL, KNIVES ARE REALLY—

"Really what?" Margo asked.

"Really sharp! Somehow that part of the sign got cut off."

Then Brock showed them his fish tank. It was full of silvery piranhas swimming around with ridiculous underbites, their

razor-sharp teeth jutting up toward the ceiling.

Shivers jumped back. "They're terrifying!"

"I could take 'em," Albee said with the bloated confidence of a blowfish.

The next stop on the tour was Brock's sword-sharpening room.

"Who needs a whole room for sword sharpening?" asked Shivers.

"That's what Billy the Blunt said."

"I've never heard of him."

"Exactly," said Brock.

The tour ended there, because they had reached New Jersey Beach. Brock dropped anchor and they hurried off the ship. As they ran onto the sand, Shivers looked back nervously at the orange sunlight skimming across the ocean. Evening was beginning to set in and he knew that the orange would soon be fading to red and not long after that, it would be nighttime. When he reached the pit in the sand where the *Land Lady* used to sit, he stopped running. He stood still, sadly realizing how empty the beach looked without his ship.

"What's wrong?" Margo asked.

"If we don't return the torch in time, this might be my last time on this beach with you."

Margo was about to say something, but instead she marched forward toward the bank.

"Where are you going?" Shivers called.

She turned around and looked him straight in the eye. "To get that torch."

The Bank of New Jersey was just a hop, skip, and a jump away from the beach, but Margo preferred running. It was much faster. Before they knew it, Shivers, Margo, and Brock had reached the magnificent white stone building. They walked through the big, glass doors into the cavernous lobby. Everything was made of marble, from the floors to the walls to the many statues of men in fancy tuxedos holding up dollar bills and drooling. The bank was crowded with people standing patiently in a long line that led to a row of bank tellers.

They quickly noticed a sign that said BANK VAULTS THIS WAY with an arrow pointing to a corridor. As they walked over to it, they were stopped by a guard who looked like a big muscly meat loaf. "Whoa, whoa, whoa, where do you think you're going?" he asked.

"Vault twenty-five," Margo said, confidently holding up the key.

"Sorry, munchkin, only adults allowed in the vaults. Despite their name, these safes are not safe."

Margo glared at him. On her list of Things She Hated, being told what to do was very high up. Being called munchkin was even higher. She turned on her heels and marched away to scope out the scene. There were guards posted throughout the room: three in front of the ATMs, two in front of the hallway that led to the vaults, and strangely, six in front of the coffee machine.

"We need to get past these guards," Margo said, still steamed.

"I've got an idea," said Brock. "I'll smash 'em!"

"You can't smash them," said Margo. "That will just draw more attention to us. We need to create a distraction."

Brock pointed at the customers. "It seems like everyone in here is already distracted. They're just standing around staring ahead at nothing. Why are they doing that?"

"They're waiting in line," Margo explained.

"Hm." Brock scratched his chin. He couldn't figure out the reason for this so-called line. "Wouldn't it be easier if they all just rushed to the front at the same time and started screaming? That's the Brock way!" He gave a thumbs-up and smiled.

Margo saw through the bank window that the sun was just bumping up against the horizon. If there was ever a time for a risk, it was now. She smiled and said, "Maybe you should show them the Brock way."

Before Shivers could protest in fear, Brock was barreling straight through the line. "ME FIRST!!!!" he screamed.

"Hey! *I* was about to be first!" shouted the woman at the front of the line.

"And *I* was going to be first after that!" shouted the man behind her.

"Does the line mean *nothing*???!!!" a man in the middle cried, shaking his fist at the sky.

Confusion swept through the crowd until one woman stood up tall and declared, "If that guy doesn't have to wait, then neither do I!"

The concept caught on quickly and the line unraveled into chaos.

"NO LINE! NO LINE! NO LINE!" the customers shouted, dashing toward the bank tellers.

It was complete pandemonium. The guards rushed away from their posts to try to get everyone under control. As soon as the coast was clear, Margo grabbed Shivers's arm and ran down the corridor toward the vaults. They took one last look back at the surging crowd.

"I told you lines were dangerous," said Shivers.

They ran down the hallway, past rows and rows of heavy locked doors. The farther they went, the more deserted the place felt. It was clear that no one came here very often. The air was damp and cold and the corners were full of dust and cobwebs. Soon, they spotted Vault 24, so Vault 25 couldn't be far. They were about to turn a corner when they heard someone cough, the sound echoing off of the marble walls. They peeked around the corner and saw a man right outside Vault 25. He had poufy white hair that looked like a dollop of whipped cream and a thick bristly mustache that looked like a fuzzy worm had crawled on his face and died. He was sitting in a splintery wooden chair, reading a magazine.

"What are we going to do?" Margo asked.

Shivers looked more closely at the magazine in the guard's hands. The cover was a picture of a pile of pillows. Shivers recognized it right away. "*Snoozer's Weekly*!" he exclaimed. "The Puffy Pillow Edition? I didn't even know that hit the stands yet! They've got a whole list of new naps in there!"

"Shivers, now is not the time for naps!" Margo said in her loudest whisper.

Margo was an expert at a lot of things—sword fighting, detective work, general awesomeness. But if there was one thing for certain that Shivers knew more about, it was naps. He turned to her and said, "It *is* the time for naps. Stay here." He turned the corner, padding softly up to the guard.

"Hey, you're not supposed to be back here!" the guard barked, jumping out of his chair.

"Yes I am! I'm from . . ." Shivers cleared his throat. "The bank's comfort department! It must be tough sitting in that chair all day. It doesn't look very comfortable."

The guard sighed. "It's not. If it weren't for the spiders keeping me company, I don't know how I'd stay awake all day."

Shivers froze. A single bead of sweat dripped off his forehead and onto the floor. (It was immediately slurped up by a spider.) But he knew he had to stay focused.

"Maybe this would make it more comfortable . . ." Shivers untied his cape and swept it along the dusty floor, gathering a pile of cobwebs and moth mold and scooping it into the cape. It was gross, but it was also very soft. He tied the cape up into a sack, making a homemade pillow. He placed it on the chair. "Why don't you try it out?"

The guard eyed him suspiciously through his thick, black-rimmed glasses, but then he sat back down. He bounced up and down, testing out the pillow. A couple of plumes of dust squeezed from the sides, but it was very comfy. "Not bad," he admitted.

As he snuggled into the pillow, Shivers could see his eyelids begin to get heavy. So he kept going.

"You know what you need?" Shivers cooed. He ran to a window and cracked it open. "The soothing sounds of the ocean." The soft sound of waves crashing in the distance floated through the hallway.

"That's nice," said the guard, a sleepy smile on his face.

The whole thing was so peaceful, Shivers let out a yawn. It was just a small one—what Shivers called a yawnlet. But he fought through it and pressed on. "What good is a pillow and some easy breezes without a blanket and something to snuggle with?" he said gently. He whisked the guard's jacket from the back of his chair and wrapped it around him, tucking him in. Then he took off his left bunny slipper, patted it on the head, and nestled it in the guard's arms. Finally, he sat down beside the chair and began to sing one of his favorite songs.

Within moments, the guard fell fast asleep, his mustache bristles ruffling with every snore. Margo tiptoed over.

"Great job, Shivers!" she whispered.

"Thanks!" he whispered as he gently took his slipper back. "Now, we just have to be really quiet—"

"What are you guys whispering about?!" Brock shouted, coming up behind them.

"Shhhh!" Margo and Shivers glared at him.

"Shivers just put that guard to sleep," Margo explained softly.

"Wow!" Brock said, a little more quietly than before. "How did you do it? Did you sing him a lullaby?"

"A lullaby?!" Shivers balked. "I hardly knew him! I sang him a lulla-hello."

"Brock, how did you get away from all those other guards?" Margo asked.

"I shouted that they were out of coffee and they ran away." Brock shrugged.

"I guess the coast is clear, then," Margo said. Then she turned to Shivers. "Would you like to do the honors?" She smiled and handed him the key to Vault 25. He took a deep breath and turned the key in the lock. With a satisfying CLICK, the door to the vault creaked open. The tiny room was filled from front to back with odds and ends from every corner of the earth. A small barred window let in a slice of sunlight, and as their eyes adjusted, they saw what was standing in the middle.

"The Treasure Torch," Shivers whispered.

"The Treasure Torch," Margo whispered.

"THE TREASURE TORCH!" Brock whispered in his softest shout.

The Treasure Torch was even more amazing than any of them had imagined. It towered over them in all its torchiness. Its shiny surface sparkled where the light hit it, sending beams of golden glow bouncing throughout the room.

They all ran into the vault. Brock pumped his fists in the air. Margo skipped around the torch with glee. Albee did a celebratory water dance.

Shivers walked right up to the torch, stretched his arms out, and hugged it as tightly as his little muscles would allow. "Hello, big guy," he whispered. "You're mine now."

But then a shadowy figure emerged from behind the door and slammed it shut. "Funny, I was going to say the same thing about you!"

They all turned to see the shimmer of three silver teeth hiding inside a crooked smile. It was Francois.

CHAPTER EIGHT

"AAAAGH! THE GHOST OF Francois!!" Shivers screamed.

"No, it's the person of Francois!" he shook his head in disbelief. "It's me!"

"AAAAAGH! That's also terrifying!"

"Welcome to my vault." Francois stepped toward them, his thin gray mustache twitching menacingly. "Where I keep my most valuable treasure." He gestured proudly toward the Treasure Torch. "Along with the gruesome artifacts that those fools at the Frank Fest couldn't even stomach. Especially this jar full of stomachs!"

He held up a murky jar.

Shivers, Margo, and Brock nervously backed away from him.

"First, you blow up my brother. And then you try to take away my most precious treasure. Now, it's time for you to pay the price," he said, advancing toward them.

Brock stepped backward, crashing into a cluster of old canary cages.

Shivers pleaded, "But I need the Treasure Torch to get my home back."

"I don't think you understand," Francois cackled. "They say home is where the heart is. Welcome to your new home!" he pointed to a basket full of dried hearts. "Time to add to my collection."

The color in Shivers's face drained away like bathwater at bedtime.

Francois rifled through a drawer, then pulled out a rusty hammer and a heart-shaped cookie cutter. "Hold still, please!"

"AAAAAAAAAGH!" Shivers darted away

from him and Margo and Brock followed.

"Quick, over here!" Shivers cried, running behind a glass case. "We'll be safe behind this display of comfy little beds!"

"Those are cockroach coffins from Caracas!" Francois bellowed as he leaped behind the case.

"AGGGHH!!" Shivers jumped as far away as he could.

Margo and Brock ran to opposite corners. Shivers tore across the vault, clutching Albee's bag so tightly he was worried it was going to pop like the beach ball.

"Under here!" he cried, diving into a pile of what looked like little black sponges. He felt them brush against his face and couldn't help but snuggle in. "Wow, these miniature pillows feel like velvet!" he said, smushing them against his cheek.

"Actually, those are dried tiger tongues from Tangiers," said Francois.

"AAAGHHHH!" Shivers burst out of the pile, flinging tiger tongues everywhere. He was out of hiding places, so he ran to the only comfy thing in sight: a tattered, yellow armchair. He curled up in it and closed his eyes, bracing himself for the worst.

"Careful in that armchair." Francois laughed. "It's made of real arms."

Shivers shot up and screamed, his feet bouncing and wiggling across the floor.

Francois chased after him. "I've got you now!" He picked up a broom and started shaking it at him.

"AGGHH! A BROOM!" Shivers screamed.

"It's not a broom, it's a rat rake from Rwanda!" Francois moved closer to Shivers, but just as he was about to rake him,

Brock appeared in the dim, dusty light. He was holding one of the old canary cages above his head. "Bye-bye, Birdie!" he said. He brought the cage down over Francois's head, stuffed him inside, and shut the door. Margo crammed a toothpick into the lock, then snapped it in half so it would stick.

"Not my turquoise toothpick!" Francois cried.

"Where's that from?" asked Shivers.

"Target. It was on sale," Francois explained. "Now, let me out! Let me out! Let me out!"

Brock stuffed a tiger tongue in Francois's mouth so he couldn't make any more noise.

Margo looked through the little window. There was still a sliver of sun hovering above the horizon, like a bald guy bobbing out at sea. "Let's get that torch back to the mayor. Time is running out."

Brock summoned up the might of all of his muscles and hoisted up the hulking Treasure Torch. "It's . . . so . . . heavy," he grunted, lumbering toward the door.

"I'll get it!" Margo said. She quickly turned the key and threw it back in her backpack. Then she pulled the door open.

Standing in the doorway, with her hands on her hips and a wry smile on her face, was Mayor President. "Fancy meeting you here," she said. She was standing in front of the same slew of interns in suits that they had seen that morning. Her photographer was at her side.

"Mayor President!" Shivers said, looking absolutely astonished. "Well, call this convenient!

Brock, you can put the torch down."

"But I just picked it up!" Brock whined, letting it drop to the ground with a crash.

"How did you find us here?" Margo asked, completely confused.

"It wasn't easy. You're a man of many mysteries, Shivers the Pirate. Or should I say . . . Shivers the Pie Man?!"

Shivers, Margo, and Albee looked at each other, baffled.

"Oh, still playing the confused card, are you?" Mayor President snapped. "This morning, you pretended you didn't know where the torch was, and now you're pretending you didn't know I was having you followed all day!"

"Followed?!" Shivers balked.

"Of course! That's why you led us on a wild-goose chase all over the Eastern Seaboard, isn't it? To try to shake our tail? But luckily, my photographer was faster than you thought. He led me straight to you." She turned to her photographer.

"Isn't that right . . . Frank? If that is your real name."

"It's not! It's still Roger!" The photographer said, ripping off a fake Frank name tag that was stuck to his shirt. Then he handed the mayor a stack of photographs. She fanned them out for Shivers and Margo to see.

"First, you tried to hide in a hallway like a wiener."

"Then, you tried to pull that Frank prank. But you walked right into our trap! And by trap, I mean photo booth!"

"Then you tried to slip away at sea! You almost lost us there, but you know what they say: 'One man's trash is another man's treasure.'"

"And now, here we are. Once you thought you'd finally lost us, you came here to move your treasure to a new hiding place. You may be a criminal mastermind, but I've got enough minds to master any pirate."

Shivers was speechless. But that was okay because Margo was speechful. She looked up at the mayor defiantly. "You've got it all wrong! Shivers isn't a criminal!"

"Oh really?! He killed that guard outside the vault!"

"He's not dead, he's just taking a really great nap!!" Shivers insisted.

"Enough with your lies! Time to take my treasure!"

"Your treasure?" Margo asked.

"I've got a few tricks up my own sleeve." Mayor President smiled. "Or should I say . . . my own pantaloons!" She ripped off her suit jacket, revealing a tattered velvet pirate coat. Then she yanked at what looked like a loose thread at her waist and her pants bunched up like curtains, transforming into billowing pantaloons. She kicked off one of her boots. Where her foot should have been, there was only the frayed wood of a rotting peg leg.

Margo and Brock screamed. Shivers was stunned. "You're not a mayor, you're a—"

"Pirate! That's right!"

Behind her, all the men and women tore off their business suits, unveiling their true appearances—hollowed eye sockets and half-eaten ears, chipped teeth and chapped lips.

"And those aren't interns, those are—"

"Pirate interns! That's right!"

"That's definitely not what I was going to guess," said Shivers.

The mayor nodded back at her mangy crew. They swarmed into the vault, lifted the Treasure Torch above their heads and scurried away like cockroaches from a lamp light.

The mayor beamed. "Now that I have the Treasure Torch, I'm the most powerful pirate in the Seven Seas! No thanks to you, Shivers."

Shivers piped up, "But Mayor President . . . or whoever you are—"

"You can still call me Mayor President. Because now I'm the mayor of the Seven Seas!" She thought for a moment. "And the president, too! And I will have any treasure I please!"

"But I never even wanted that torch! I just wanted my home back."

"You know, they say home is where the heart is . . ."

Shivers sighed. "Again? You've got to be kidding me."

"YOU LIVE HERE NOW!" She busted out a belly laugh made of pure evil. "I can't have such a clever pirate sailing the Eastern Seas, trying to plunder my treasure."

Shivers trembled in his bunny slipper as more pirate interns flooded into the vault, blocking the path to the door.

Brock shook his head. The gears inside were moving, but just a little too slowly. "I don't understand. I thought she was a mayor!"

"Things aren't always what they seem." She glanced around the vault and noticed Francois, still inside the birdcage. "Just like this canary appears to be a man. I will take him as my pet."

A group of pirate interns carried Francois out.

The mayor turned to leave, but then she whirled around to face them once again. "And one more thing, I need an intern to sift through the seaweed on my new pirate ship. Someone spunky. With small hands. Who can sleep in a slop bucket." She pointed at Margo. "She'll do."

"SHIVERS!" Margo screamed as four grizzled pirates scooped her up. "HELP!!"

But all he could do was yelp. "MARGO!!!!"

One of the pirates took off Margo's green backpack and tossed it to the floor. The silver key tumbled out. The mayor plucked it up and threw it like a dart across the vault and out the barred

window. Shivers froze in a stunned silence until he heard the soft PLINK! of the key landing outside.

"Have a super-amazing day!" the mayor said.

Shivers and Brock rushed to get out, but before they could even take two steps, the pirates whisked Margo away and the mayor slammed the vault door with a

SMACK!

CHAPTER NINE

"NO!!!!" SHIVERS SHOUTED, HIS face so full of horror it looked like he had just gulped a gallon of sour milk.

"I'll get us out!" Brock shouted. He charged at the door headfirst and smacked into it, falling onto the floor in a heap. The door didn't budge. Plus, it opened inward, so it really wasn't a great idea from the get-go. "Ow," he said, rubbing the big, red lump that was forming where his blond hair met his goofy face.

"Help!! Let us out!!" Shivers screamed, but no one answered. The only person around was the guard, but apparently he was still sleeping. Shivers bitterly kicked the door. "Why do I have to be so good at lulling people into cozy naps?! We're going to be stuck in here forever!"

"You mean . . . we're bankers now?" This time it was Brock who was horrified.

"No! Brock! We're trapped! By the time anyone finds us, we'll be dried up like a couple of tiger tongues! And Albee will be nothing but a fish fossil! The poor guy hasn't eaten since this morning!"

Brock picked a tin can up from one of the shelves. "Look! Here's a can of fish flakes! Albee can have a little snack!"

Shivers grabbed the can and read the label aloud. "'Fish Flakes from Finland. Made from One Hundred Percent Dead Fish.'"

Albee was absolutely appalled.

In a fit of frustration, Shivers chucked the can across the vault. It exploded against the wall in a plume of fishy dust.

"Don't worry, little brother, we'll figure out something!"

"When?! How?! Margo needs us right now. The worst part of all this isn't that we're stuck in here, it's that she's stuck out there, sleeping in President Psycho's slop bucket! And it's all my fault!" He slumped to the floor, feeling more crushed than a can kicked down a canyon. Albee tried to pat him on the shoulder, but he just couldn't reach.

"It's not your fault," Brock insisted. "It's Mayor President's fault for being such a bad mayor! Or . . . such a good pirate! I'm still so confused." He scratched his head. "Still, there's got to be a way to smash out of here."

Shivers didn't answer. He just stared glumly out the window. And that gave Brock an idea.

"Hey, maybe I could cram you through those window bars!!"

"What?!"

But before Shivers could protest any more, Brock hoisted him onto his hulking shoulders and carried him over to the window. Shivers gripped the bars to steady himself.

"Now think like a juicer and squeeze!" Brock screamed, pushing Shivers in the pantaloons.

Shivers's face smushed against the bars. Brock pushed harder, but Shivers's head was much too big to fit through. "It's not going to work, Brock! My head is too big."

But then, out of the corner of his eye, Shivers spied a glint of metal. He gasped so hard he nearly choked. "The key!" he said. "It's down there!" The key was caught in the branches of a bush at the base of the bank building.

"Grab it!!" Brock urged.

Shivers stuck his scrawny arm through the bars and grasped for the key but his hands came up emptier than his post-breakfast popcorn bowl. "I can't get it! It's too far away!"

"Let me try! I've got longer arms than you!" Brock said, setting Shivers back down on the floor. Shivers breathed a sigh of relief.

"Stand still. Coming up!" Brock said. Shivers immediately unbreathed the sigh of relief and sucked in a gasp of fear as Brock jumped onto his shoulders. They came crashing to the floor before Albee could even say "Timber!"

Brock brushed himself off, but Shivers stayed on the floor in a puddle of misery. Even though the key was right outside, they were just as trapped as ever. "If Margo were here, she'd know what to do," he whimpered.

"Would she tell you to stop weeping like a willow and feeling sorry for yourself?" Brock snapped.

Shivers thought for a moment. "I think she'd tell me that bravery comes from within. But I don't know what that means."

"Maybe it means from within her backpack!" Brock picked up Margo's big green backpack, which had been on the floor of the vault ever since the pirates took her away. Brock unzipped it and turned it upside down. Everything inside came tumbling out: a pack of pencils, a green bandanna, a yellow banana, an old stick, a fish stick, and a pile of other stuff that Brock didn't even notice because he was fixated on one thing: The yo-yo from Frank Fest with an *F* on both sides. He picked it up and tried to hand it to Shivers. "You can use it to hook the key!"

"Get that away from me!" Shivers cried. "It's like a baby boomerang! Those things should be illegal!"

"It's the only way out!" Brock insisted.

Shivers was uneasy. Anything that could escape gravity like that was clearly the work of witches or ghosts or both. He decided to ask his first mate.

Shivers crouched down next to Albee's bag. "What do you think?"

"Well, I think it looks pretty easy," Albee said.

"What's that? You think it's really scary and difficult but it might be the only way to save my best nonfish friend?! You always know just what to say." Shivers took a deep breath. "Let's do it."

Brock planted his feet and Shivers shimmied back up onto his shoulders. Albee supervised. Once Shivers reached the window, Brock handed him the yo-yo and he hooked it onto his finger. As soon as he saw it in his hand he screamed and dropped it, but it flew back up. "Witchcraft!!" he squealed. He tried to get rid of it again but it bounced back toward him like a toy on a mission. "Get it off me! Get it off me!" he squawked, throwing the yo-yo down over and over again, narrowly missing Brock's head.

"Shivers!" Brock shouted. "Try throwing it out the window!"

"Begone, yo-yo!" Shivers cried, raising up his

hand. He flung the yo-yo as hard as he could through the bars of the window. It swooped down along the side of the wall, then hit the bush and hooked onto the key. Then, with the force of a thousand yo's, it barreled up and back through the bars, flinging the key into the vault, where it dropped to the floor right next to Albee's bag.

"Got it!" said Albee.

Shivers scampered down from Brock's shoulders as fast as he could, then lay down on the floor, kissed it, and whispered, "I'll never leave you again."

Brock picked up the key and unlocked the door. Shivers got Margo's bag, and then he got Albee's bag, and then he got out of that bank as fast as he possibly could.

CHAPTER TEN

BROCK STOOD IN THE crow's nest of *Solid as a Brock*, looking through a pair of pirate binoculars—which were just like regular binoculars except they had an eye patch over one side.

"Any sign of them?" Shivers called up from the deck. He was in a panic over which way to sail.

"Nothing yet!" Brock said, spinning around like the lamp on a lighthouse. "All I see is a big party boat, a cargo ship, and—" He adjusted the binoculars to get a closer look. "The *Land Lady*?! What's that doing out at sea?"

"WHAT?! My *Land Lady*?!"

"It sure is," Brock said, looking at the name written on the side of the ship. "But it's got a lot more cannons than it used to."

"You mean more than zero?" Shivers asked.

"A *lot* more than zero. And the Treasure Torch is right there on the deck!"

"What?! Give me those!"

Brock tossed the binoculars down to Shivers. He looked through them, spotted the *Land Lady*, then zeroed in on the helm. Steering his ship was Mayor President. "Follow that *Land Lady*!!!" Shivers shouted.

"You got it!" Brock raised up the anchor and they sped across the water. Under the dark night sky, the ocean was rough and the waves were chopping more than a kung fu movie. Luckily, *Solid as a Brock* was a much stronger and faster ship than the *Land Lady*, so they gained ground quickly—or, rather, they gained sea quickly. As they got closer, Shivers looked through the binoculars again. There was no sign of Margo but he could see that the mayor was surrounded by her menacing pirate crew.

"I don't think we can do this alone," Shivers said nervously.

"I know! I'll call Mom and Dad!"

"You have a phone on your ship?" Shivers asked.

Brock laughed heartily. "Who needs a phone? Phones are so last century." He ran to the back deck of the ship, cleared his throat and bellowed. "HEY, MOM! HEY, DAD!"

Brock's voice was so loud that it echoed all the way back to New Jersey Beach and through the town. One by one, moms and dads popped their heads out their windows, calling, "Yes, dear?"

"Sorry!" Brock shouted. He knew he would have to be more specific. "TILDA! BOB!" But there was no answer. Brock shrugged. "I guess I'll leave a message. WE'RE GOING INTO BATTLE! HELP!"

But there was no time to wait for a response. They had just drifted into the *Land Lady*'s wake. Now, Shivers was able to really see what the mayor had done to his ship. His mop collection had been replaced with seventeen sharp swords. His flag had been replaced with a new one that was just a giant picture of the mayor's snarling face. Even his coat hooks had been replaced with real hooks, which just seemed unnecessary. And Brock really wasn't kidding about the cannons. They were everywhere. A group of pirate interns patrolled the deck, filling each cannon with thick, gray goop.

At that moment, a huge wave from Brock's ship rocked the *Land Lady*. The mayor turned around in surprise and spotted them. She rushed furiously onto the deck. "You escaped!" she screeched into her megaphone. "Another masterful move from Shivers the Pirate. Well, there's no escaping now." She pointed one of the cannons directly at them, and her interns followed suit with the rest. "I realize that if I can't outsmart you, I'll just have to make you fish food."

"What have you done to my *Land Lady*?!" Shivers cried.

"I knew that if I was going to become the most powerful pirate on the seas, I would need a powerful pirate ship. So when I took it from you this morning I had my crew redecorate. All they had to do was get my old pirate gear out of storage!"

"*Old* pirate gear?" Brock asked. "Can someone please explain to me who this lady is?"

"I suppose there's time for one more story before you get slurped up by the great blue stew."

She laughed, gesturing wildly at the ocean. "I was born at sea, you see. But no matter how much treasure I plundered, I never had any power. I was a Nobody! Seriously! My name was Sheila B. Nobody! So what did I do? I left my pirate life, moved on land, and gave myself the most power-ful name I could think of. Before I knew it, I was the most powerful person in all of New Jersey. I got a free house and free cars! And all the interns I could stuff into an office! But I wanted more! Once I discovered that the Treasure Torch was out there and that you were keeping it from me, I knew the time had come for me to return to the sea. And look at me now! I retrained my interns to be perfect pirates, I have my very own ship, and the Treasure Torch is mine. There's no pirate more powerful than me. And you're not going to stand in my way anymore!"

"Oh, I get it now." Brock nodded. "You really gave us the long version, huh?"

The mayor glowered at him. "Then I'll make

the rest of this quick. Good-bye, Shivers! It was terrible knowing you!" She raised up her fist and brought it down onto a red button at the base of the cannon. There was a thunderous BOOM! as it fired directly at them.

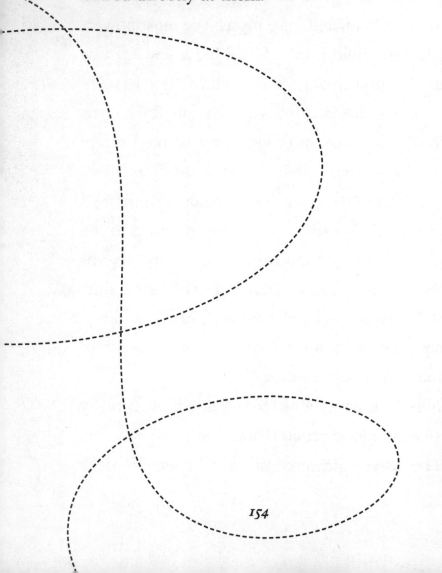

CHAPTER ELEVEN

SPLURRSH! THE CANNON SHOT landed on Brock's ship, spraying a mountainous mixture of moldy gloop across the deck. Shivers had no idea what had just been shot out of the cannon, but whatever it was, it gave him the willies.

"What *is* that stuff?" Shivers asked, sticking out his tongue in disgust. "It looks like sewer slime!"

Brock examined a glob of slop on his deck. "And it smells like guacamole."

The mayor cackled from the captain's deck. "It's cafeteria food!" she announced proudly, her voice blasting from the megaphone. "I didn't have any cannonballs, but as mayor I had unlimited access to the elementary school's leftovers. I took one look at this stuff and thought, this is way more dangerous than cannonballs! See?"

She signaled to the pirate interns and they all fired their cannons at once. A deadly deluge rained onto Brock's ship. This time, the rotten food hit with such force that it splintered the hull. Another round of cannonfire hit, and the back of *Solid as a Brock* cracked in half.

"Uh-oh. I guess I have to rename it *Sinking Like a Brock*. Abandon ship!" Brock cried. He saw that Shivers was still wearing Margo's backpack and decided to pull Shivers onto his own back. Shivers wrapped his arms around Brock's shoulders and held Albee's bag tightly in his hands.

"You can swim, right?" Brock asked, leaping over the railing.

But before Shivers could scream, "NO!" they plunged into the blackness below.

Shivers wanted to kick and thrash in a panic, but the water was so cold that he just stayed frozen to Brock's back as he fought against the waves. Brock made it to the *Land Lady* and tried to grab on to the ship, but his hands slipped off the slimy wooden sides. Just then, he saw something drop down from Shivers's bedroom porthole. It looked like a rope covered in soggy green leaves. "Wow, your daisies have really grown long," he said. Shivers tried to warn Brock that daisies don't look like that but his mouth was too full of freezing salt water to do anything but shiver and spit.

Brock pulled them

up onto the rope and started a steady climb toward the porthole. He took one last look over his shoulder just in time to see his old ship, which had *just* been his new ship, slip beneath the surface of the sea. "I hope my piranhas are okay," he said.

"I can't say I agree," Albee replied.

But there was no time for arguments. Brock had reached the porthole. He hoisted Shivers and Albee inside, then squeezed himself through the small, circular window like a raccoon through a Ring Pop. Finally, there was a POP! like a cork being pulled out of a bottle as Brock pushed himself all the way through. He landed on his back next to Shivers on the floor of the bedroom.

Staring down at them, holding the rope, was the friendliest, most fearless face they could hope to find.

"Margo!" Shivers exclaimed, leaping up from the floor and dancing around her. "I'm so happy to see you! I'm so happy you're safe! I'm so—" He glanced around his bedroom and saw that it was covered in ocean garbage. "DISGUSTED!!! What happened to my room?!"

"The mayor turned it into the seaweed-sifting station. I have to sit here and sort through all this filth looking for hidden treasure." Among the muck was a pile of thick gold chains covered in slime that had been scraped from the sea floor. The pile was almost as tall as Margo. "But on the plus side, when I heard all the commotion and saw you guys outside I was able to drop you a line!" She held the seaweed rope up proudly.

Shivers took off Margo's backpack and handed it to her. "I thought you might be missing this."

"My backpack!" Margo was thrilled. She opened it up and gobbled down the banana and the fish stick. "I was starving."

"So what do we do now?" Brock asked.

"I have to clean up this mess," said Shivers. "I hope the mayor didn't find my spare mop." He opened his closet and took out the most enormous mop any of them had ever seen.

"There's no time for cleaning! We only have two options here. It's fight or flight," Margo said.

Shivers shook the mop in frustration. "How many times do I have to tell you guys, I'm afraid of heights!"

Margo's eyes sharpened like two green colored pencils. "Then I guess it's fight."

"Finally!" Brock shouted. "Brock smash!" He charged headfirst through Shivers's door, breaking it off its hinges as he ran into the hallway.

"Get ahold of yourself!" Shivers groaned. "Or at least get ahold of the doorknob." Margo threw her backpack on and ran after Brock. Shivers followed behind, his mop in one hand and Albee in the other.

They ran into the kitchen and looked through the porthole out onto the main deck. There were interns standing at attention behind each cannon and a circle of them guarding the Treasure Torch, which sat squarely in the center of the deck.

They heard the mayor just above them on the captain's deck, barking into her megaphone. "Interns! Why are you standing around? Jump in the water and sift through that ship wreckage. There's sure to be treasure down there somewhere. And if you see anybody floating around, tie a rock to their foot! Now hurry up, the freezing seawater isn't getting any warmer!"

The interns saluted her and dove straight off the deck, each one letting out a high pitched yelp when they hit the icy water. Margo raised her fist in the air and yelled, "Now's our chance! Charge! . . . I mean, CHARRRRRRGE!"

Mayor President spotted them and was so

shocked that she dropped her megaphone. It fell from the captain's deck and landed with a clatter on the main deck. The mayor howled, "You again!! Interns, assemble!!"

In an instant, a new group of interns rushed onto the deck. It was hard to imagine that just hours ago they were wearing cleanly pressed suits, since now they looked like they had crawled out of a sewer. Their hands were caked with mud from seaweed sifting and their rotten teeth were speckled with popcorn kernels.

"My popcorn!" Shivers shouted, appalled.

But the mayor's voice overpowered his as she yelled at the crew, "Seize the stowaways! Stick them in seaweed and simmer them over the stove! Alliterate and obliterate them! And remember, protect me at all costs and one day you might get paid for this job!"

The interns swarmed but the first one to reach them was the mayor's photographer, Roger. He shot them with the only weapon he had—his camera. He blinded Shivers, Margo, and Brock with a bright flash. "Aggh! A photobomb!" Shivers shrieked. They tried to push past Roger, but all the pops of bright light made it impossible to see where they were going. Brock had been in enough fistfights during lightning storms to know how to handle the situation. He closed his eyes and barreled forward. And when he opened his eyes, he was behind the photographer's back. He called out, "Hey, snappy! Picture this!" The photographer spun around with just enough time to capture the moment.

"I guess it's lights-out for that guy," said Albee, but no one was paying attention.

Once their eyes adjusted, they saw that the pirates were all around them with their rusty swords and trusty daggers ready to strike.

"Stay back!" Shivers stammered, holding his mop above his head.

"What are you going to do with that?" Brock asked.

"I'll . . . scrub them clean?" Shivers tried.

Brock just sighed and shook his head.

Shivers looked at Albee with terrified eyes. "Well, I guess this is the end. Promise you won't eat me when I turn into fish food."

"It's not the end," Margo said, her eyes as strong as steel. "We just have to stick together."

"Yeah!" Brock cheered. "Pirates stick together! Like . . . two sticks . . . in a pile of sticks!" Sometimes Brock had trouble describing things.

A pirate intern with a hook hand and a hooked

nose lunged at Margo with his sword, trying to slice her like a ham sandwich. She jumped back and something caught her eye in the reflection of his blade. It was the mayor's bright orange megaphone, sitting on the deck just behind her. In an instant, her big beautiful brain knew exactly what to do. She tapped Shivers on the shoulder and said, "There's something I have to tell you."

"What is it?" he asked, backing up against the wall and clutching the mop for dear life.

Margo looked him square in the eye and said, "Popcorn is really made from parrot poop."

Shivers gasped. His face turned pale as he thought about all the popcorn he had eaten in his life. If it's true that you are what you eat, then Shivers was made of mostly parrot poop. Just as he opened his mouth to scream, Margo scooped up the megaphone and held it in front of him.

"AAAAAAAAAAAGGGGGGGGGHHH!!!!!"
Shivers wailed. The megaphone blasted the sound
into the interns' faces, blowing back their hair
and beating against their eardrums. They covered their ears, turned, and scurried away from
the shrieking. They huddled closely together at
the end of the ship's deck and crammed their fingers in their ears to keep the screams out.

Margo dropped the megaphone, turned to Shivers, and said, "Just kidding!"

"Don't scare me like that!" He breathed a sigh of relief. "Hey, where did everybody go?"

Then, to everyone's surprise, there was a thundering shout. "BROCK SMASH!!!"

With the force of a giant bowling ball, Brock plowed head first, body second, feet third into the crew. It was like a flying bear hug. The railing cracked behind them and the whole mass of bodies flew overboard into the churning waves below.

Shivers and Margo rushed to the edge of the deck and searched the water for any sign of Brock. The sea was full of bobbing heads but they were all thrashing around so much it was impossible to tell them apart.

Shivers called out, hoping Brock would hear, "Stay there! We'll throw you a life jacket!"

"Don't you mean a *death* jacket??!!"

Margo and Shivers gasped and turned around. Standing dangerously close to them was Francois.

"A death jacket? That's not a real thing!" Margo insisted.

"It is so! I got one in Denmark!" Francois replied. His back was now as crooked as his smile after being trapped in the canary cage.

He took a step toward them and they inched away until their heels reached the edge of the deck with their backs facing the open ocean.

Shivers gripped Margo's hand, his eyes ablaze with panic. "What are we going to do?!"

"For once, Shivers the Pirate doesn't know what to do," the mayor said, leisurely descending from the captain's deck. She sauntered up next to Francois. "I see you've met my partner in crime. You can imagine my surprise when I found out that my new pet wasn't a canary dressed like a man, but a man living like a canary. It turns out we have a lot in common."

"That's right!" said Francois. "We both enjoy long walks on the beach, and our favorite ice-cream flavor is bubble gum. We've never been to Hawaii but we'd like to go someday–"

"TREASURE! I meant treasure."

Francois smacked his forehead. "Of course. And now, together we're going to snatch the treasure from every hand, hook, and set of false teeth in the seas."

"Any pirate who doesn't give us their treasure gets a cannonful of cafeteria casserole. How's that for a master plan, Shivers the Pirate Mastermind?" the mayor said with a satisfied smile.

"For the last time, I'm not a pirate mastermind!!" Shivers insisted.

"That's just what a mastermind would say! If you're not an amazing pirate, then how did you craft a raft out of beach balls?"

"Margo did that. Personally, I don't like to go anywhere near anything that has to get blown up," Shivers explained.

"How did you fight off an angry mob of Franks?"

"That was all Margo's pillow-fighting skills. Believe me, you do *not* want to invite this girl to a slumber party." Shivers pointed at her and she smiled sheepishly.

"How did you plunder the Treasure Torch and keep it hidden in your secret bank vault?" the mayor asked.

"That wasn't their secret bank vault, it was my secret bank vault!" said Francois. "I hid the torch there and they found it!"

The mayor's face started to twitch uncontrollably. "BUT HOW?!"

Shivers shrugged. "Ask Margo."

The mayor's eyes zeroed in on Margo like she was the bull's-eye on a target. "So *you're* the real mastermind," she sneered. "Well, I hope you enjoyed sifting through seaweed because soon it'll be the seaweed that's sifting through *you.*" She took a threatening step toward her.

"No!" Shivers cried, horrified that he had set the mayor's sights on Margo. "Don't push her in the ocean!"

The mayor chuckled. "Oh, I won't. I've got a much more permanent solution." She grabbed Margo's arm and started dragging her away.

"What should I do with him?" Francois asked, gesturing to Shivers. "Kick him in the ocean and then dump his fish on land?"

"Him?" The mayor thought for a moment. "Make him an intern—for life! He can start by reloading the cannons. Keep an eye on him and another eye on his fish." She smiled. "It's so nice to have a pirate partner with two working eyes." Then she yanked Margo toward the other side of the ship and out of Shivers's sight.

Francois pulled a jewel-encrusted dagger from a sheath at his hip. He pointed it at Shivers and commanded, "Drop the mop, ditch the fish, and start cramming cannons." He marched over to a huge barrel next to a nearby cannon. He kicked

over the barrel, spilling out a cluster of cans full of food for a cafeteria casserole. There were Grated Gray Beans in Grease, Triple Trashed Potatoes in Gravy, Mixed Mystery Meats in Marinara, and worst of all, Canned Clams in Curdled Cream.

Shivers shuddered. The memory of this morning's clam clamping catastrophe was still fresh in his mind. In fact, it was the only fresh thing around. But he had to listen to Francois. He let the mop slip from his grip and set Albee down gently on the deck. "You supervise," he said sadly. Then he trudged over to the pile of food and got to work. He opened a can of gray beans and poured them into the cannon, but his hands were shaking from fear. He accidentally splashed grease all over the ground.

"I saw that!" Francois snarled. "You'd better shape up. Soon you'll be the only crew member on this ship."

Terror washed over Shivers. He couldn't help but think about Brock churning like ice cream in the water below, and he didn't want to think about what the mayor might do to Margo. He tried to calm down by telling himself Margo's advice: "Bravery comes from within."

Bravery comes from within? Bravery comes from within . . . Bravery. Comes. From. Within.

Shivers picked up the clams. He cracked open the can, closed his eyes, and poured the clams straight down his throat.

CHAPTER TWELVE

THE CANNED CLAMS IN Curdled Cream hit Shivers with a quadruple strength *C*-sickness. They bubbled through his body, mixing and mashing with half-chewed hot dogs into the slimiest stew any pirate has ever spewed. He turned to face Francois, whose eyes bugged out of his head with disgust. Then, what came from within Shivers wasn't bravery exactly—a shower of puke flew toward Francois with the force of a fire hydrant. It landed on him with a SPLAT that sent him stumbling backward. He grasped for the ship's railing but Brock's smashing had sent that to sea long ago, so he toppled straight off the deck. As Francois fell through the air, he flapped his arms wildly and for a moment, he wished he really was a canary. But then, as he hit the water, he just wished he was a man who knew how to swim.

Shivers was exhausted but relieved. He scooped up Albee and said, "I guess it should be me who's clapping for the clams now!"

Albee blew happy bubbles in his bag.

"There's no time to chat, Albee, we've got to go find Margo!" said Shivers.

Suddenly, they heard a scream from the back of the ship.

"Margo!!!" Shivers picked up his mop and charged toward the sound. He ran around the

Treasure Torch, past the galley and the seaweed-sifting station, all the way to the other end of the ship. He arrived just in time to see that his worst nightmare was coming true—no, not the one where his bunny slippers turn into giant snails—the one where Margo is in terrible trouble. The mayor had tied her to the base of the sail and was now pointing an enormous cannon directly at her.

"No escaping now, mastermind!" the mayor cackled, loading buckets of old, cold nacho cheese into the cannon.

Margo struggled to break free but the knots were too tight. "You'll pay for this!" she bellowed.

"I won't pay for anything again! I'll just steal from pirates!" the mayor replied. "Now, I hope the fish are hungry for Margo-roni and cheese!"

She gleefully raised her finger and brought it down toward the button at the base of the cannon.

"NO!" Shivers screamed. He ran toward the mayor, raised his giant mop high above his head, and threw it. It hurtled through the air like a javelin with hair and crammed into the cannon just as the mayor pressed the button.

And just like her plan, the cannon backfired. The mop had completely clogged the cannon's barrel, and the force of the explosion shattered its heavy metal base. The force rocketed downward like a bolt of lightning blasting through the *Land Lady*. Shivers covered his face as shards of ship and chunks of cheese whizzed past him.

Then, there was a deafening SNAP! The wooden base of the ship bristled and broke in half, sending Shivers and Albee soaring across what was left of the deck. Shivers rolled until he hit the railing, then scrambled back up and over to Margo, who was still tied to the sail.

"Shivers!" Margo screamed in disbelief. "Your *Land Lady*–"

"Is not very happy with me right now! I know!" He started to untie her. Suddenly, the back end of the ship began to tilt downward and slowly sink. They both gripped the sail tightly.

The blast had knocked the mayor to the deck and she was only now able to drag herself up using the jagged edge of the broken railing. As the *Land Lady* leaned farther into the water, piles of stolen jewelry tumbled out through the port-hole of Shivers's bedroom and slid down the deck. "My treasure!" the mayor cried, chasing after the glints of gold. She looped as many bracelets as she could onto her wrists. She snatched up armfuls of sparkling chains and draped them around her neck. She clutched a chest full of copper coins.

Shivers had just finished untying Margo when the ship slanted even farther. The sail leaned completely backward like a giant hammock as it plummeted toward the water. Margo held on to the sail, Shivers held on to Margo, and Albee just held on to a grudge that he had been dragged along on this adventure in the first place.

The mayor looked up in a panic. With hor-ror, she realized the Treasure Torch was on the "Land" half of the ship, but they were on the "Lady" half. And both halves were sinking fast. "MY TORCH!" she wailed. She stretched out her arms, her heavy jewelry clanging wildly. She tried to take a step toward the torch but the treasure she was wearing weighed more than a Pig-Out Palace platter and she started to slide down the deck.

Shivers, Margo, and Albee watched in shock as the mayor skidded right past them and plunged into the water. Trapped under her treasure, she sank straight down and didn't stop until she planted on the sea floor . . . right next to Brock's piranhas.

Shivers shook his head. "I guess you really *can* go overboard with accessories."

But then he went back to

screaming as the freezing seawater hit the sail. "What are we going to do?!" he cried.

"I don't know!!" Margo said. She tried to scoop out the water with her hands but it was seeping in too quickly.

They locked terrified eyes and realized that for the first time, neither of them had a solution.

Suddenly, Shivers got hit in the face with the seaweed rope. Holding the other end was Brock. He was thrashing through the waves, kicking his way toward them.

"Brock!!" Shivers was ecstatic.

"You're okay!" said Margo.

"And you're here to save us!" said Shivers.

"I thought you were here to save me!" Brock hollered. "Grab the rope!"

Shivers and Margo gripped the rope tightly, but they were sinking just as fast as Brock.

"AAAAGGH!" Shivers screamed as the frigid seawater flooded over the edges of the sail.

Margo looked to her friends. "If we're going

down, we're going down together."

But they didn't go down, they went up. An enormous anchor rose from the water below and hooked onto the seaweed rope. As it lifted the rope by its center, Shivers, Margo, Albee, and Brock dangled from the sides like ornaments on a tree. They were raised higher and higher until they

reached the name painted on the side of the ship. It was the *Plunderer.*

"Sorry we're late!" Bob called from the deck above. Tilda was at his side, pulling up the anchor.

"Actually, you're just in time!" Shivers said. Then he looked at the scattered wreckage of the *Land Lady.* "Well, you could have been a little earlier."

They reached the deck and hopped over the railing. Except for Shivers, whose bunny slippers were so soaking wet that he had to flop over the railing.

Shivers hugged both his parents tightly, then looked to Bob. "Hey, you think you could grab one more thing with that anchor?"

"Shivers, I think you're going to need to buy a new microwave," said Tilda.

"It's a little heavier than that." Shivers smiled at Margo.

"It's the Treasure Torch!!" Brock cheered.

Bob and Tilda stared at Shivers and Margo in astonishment. Then Bob patted Shivers on the shoulder. "You found the Treasure Torch! Why am I not surprised?"

Shivers blushed. "Well, then I lost it again."

Bob nodded. "Also not surprised. Come on, let's go fishing!" He dropped the anchor back into the ocean.

Tilda put her arm around Shivers. "So, now that your ship is gone, what do you say you live out here with us? After today, you must have a taste for adventure on the high seas!"

"The only taste I have right now is curdled clams. Could somebody *please* get me a bowl of popcorn??!!!"

"All we have is sizzled squid heads," said Tilda.

Shivers grimaced. "I have to get back to my beach. It's where I belong." Shivers and Margo smiled at each other. "Plus, I've always said Albee is more of a land fish. Dad, will you build me a new ship?"

"Sure! Nothing could be as grueling as building that unsinkable ship I made for Brock!"

"Uh, Dad . . . about that . . ." But before Brock could deliver the bad news about his ship, the anchor hooked the Treasure Torch. They hauled it up out of the water and lifted it onto the deck, where it landed with an enormous THUD.

Uncle Marvin hobbled out of his sleeping quarters, tired-eyed and droopy-lipped. "What's all that racket?! I was taking a snooze in my bean bag!" Then he saw the torch towering above him and gasped. "So you solved the clue."

"We sure did!" Margo said proudly.

"I'd give you a hug if I wasn't covered in bean juice. And if I didn't hate hugging people," Marvin grumbled. "What are you going to do with it?"

Shivers thought for a moment. "I'm going to return it."

"You found the treasure that every pirate wants and no pirate can find, and now you're going to return it?!" Marvin screeched.

Shivers nodded.

Marvin sighed. "Why am I not surprised?"

CHAPTER THIRTEEN

THE TREASURE TORCH WAS safely back in Lady Liberty's hand and Shivers was sitting just below it, with Albee and Margo at his side. A huge, cheering crowd had gathered on the ground. From all the way up at the top of the statue, the people looked no bigger than crumbs. But Shivers didn't know that, since he was way too scared to look down.

Margo patted the torch.

"Are you sure you want to return this?"

Shivers replied, "I don't need it. I find it hard to believe a piece of treasure could make you all that powerful anyway." He gestured out at the celebrating crowd. "Plus, how could I expect all these people to sleep without a night light?"

Margo looked up at the night sky, the Treasure Torch casting a golden glow over the darkness. Far in the distance, she could see all that remained of Shivers's old ship: some broken wooden planks, a tattered flag, and a few unsinkable rubber duckies.

"I can't believe you blew up the *Land Lady*," said Margo.

"It's okay. What good is a home without a best friend to visit it?"

Margo smiled. "So as soon as your new ship is built, we can have–"

"Song and dance time?!" Shivers asked hopefully.

"I was going to say another terrifying adventure."

"Well"–he narrowed his eyes–"Now that you

mention it, there's a new flavor at the ice-cream shop called 'Boo Berry' that I've been particularly scared of trying, and I could really use your help."

"I think we can handle it," said Margo.

Albee smiled and nodded. "I'll supervise," he said. And he was pretty sure they understood.

THE END!

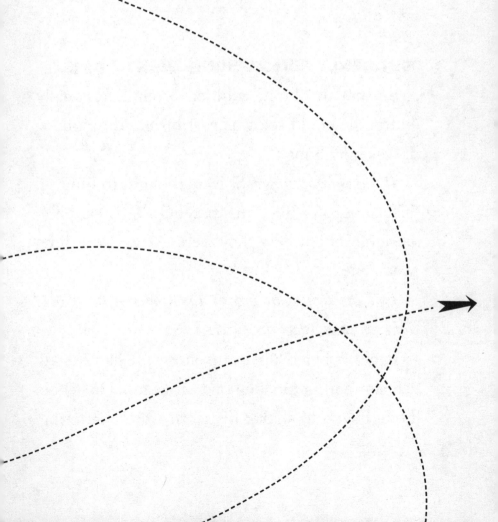

Read a shivery sneak peek of

SHIVERS!

Book III

CHAPTER ONE

SUDDENLY, EVERYTHING WENT DARK.

Shivers the Pirate whirled around frantically but all he could see was vast black nothingness. It was horrifying!

What is happening?! Shivers thought to himself. Just moments ago, his parents were standing beside him but now they were gone. Everything was gone!

Did the lightbulbs break? Did the sun burn out? Did somebody steal my eyes?!

Panic bubbled up in his stomach like a stew left simmering too long on a stove top. His whole body began to shake: his teeth were chattering, his arms were wiggling, the bunny slippers on his feet were doing a danger dance.

Where had all the light gone? Was he dreaming? Was he *nightmaring*? No, this had a for-real feel.

Shivers had spent his whole life trying to stay away from the dark and now it was all he could see. He reached out in front of him, trying to find a light to turn on. But there was nothing there. His heart pounded in his chest so wildly it sounded like it was trying to tell a knock-knock joke.

There was only one thing he could do.

"AAAAAAAGH!" Shivers shrieked. He spun around in a circle then collapsed to the ground in a screap—which, if you don't already know, is a screaming heap.

Suddenly, all the light came flooding back. Shivers was lying in the sand on New Jersey Beach. His parents, Bob and Tilda, were standing above him. His mom was holding a bandanna in her hand.

"I told you the blindfold was a bad idea," said Bob, shaking his head.

"I thought it would make the surprise more fun," said Tilda.

"What surprise?" Shivers asked suspiciously. He hated anything unexpected and generally lived by the rule "Surprises cause demises."

"*This* surprise!" Tilda said, yanking him to his feet and turning him around. Towering right in front of him was a brand-new pirate ship. It was magnificent. The polished wooden hull shimmered in the sunlight. The crisp white sails fluttered majestically in the breeze. There was even a ring of floaties surrounding the deck.

"For me?!" Shivers asked.

Tilda nodded.

"My new ship!" he shouted with glee. "It's *finally* finished! I thought I'd *never* move back to my beautiful beach!" He picked up two handfuls of sand and kissed each of them. "It's been *years*!"

Really, it had only been three days, but Shivers

had been so uneasy and so queasy that it felt like much longer. When his old ship, the *Landlady*, was destroyed, Shivers was forced to move out to sea with his parents. Bob and Tilda tried their best to make Shivers comfortable on their ship, but everything about it terrified him to the core. He wailed at every wave that rocked the ship and screamed at every seagull swooping by. Bob couldn't even toast the bread for a tuna melt without Shivers having a tuna meltdown. Shivers had a deep fear of toasters—they always pop up when you least expect it.

With all the screaming that was going on, Bob and Tilda hadn't slept a wink. They knew they had to get Shivers out of the sea and back to the beach as fast as pirately possible. Luckily, Bob was an expert shipbuilder and Tilda was an expert at plundering all of Shivers's favorite things.

Shivers burst through the front door of the ship and squealed, "It's perfect!"

Bob and Tilda showed him all around the ship.

His sleeping quarters were cozier than ever. He had brand-new curtains covered in pictures of kittens sitting in coffee cups. On top of his bed were hundreds of marshmallows sewn together to make the comfiest comforter imaginable. It also came in handy as a midnight snack.

Shivers had just one question. "Where are the night-lights?"

"Where *aren't* the night-lights?" Tilda replied. She flicked a switch and the walls lit up with floor-to-ceiling night-lights, filling the entire room with a warm glow.

"Yes!" Shivers screamed. "Death to darkness!" He ran down the hall cheering. Which was a nice change, because usually he ran down the hall fearing.

In just a few short steps, he reached his brand-new kitchen. Waiting for him on the counter was his first mate, Albee.

"Albee!" Shivers cheered. "Can you believe this place?"

He looked around the kitchen, which was customized for all of his cravings. He flung open the fridge door and found it fully stocked with his favorite soft snacks from jars of Jell-O to plates of pudding.

The pantry was packed with all kinds of mixes: brownie, pancake, and even trail. Albee had his own shelf, which was stacked with soft butter, his absolute favorite food.

Shivers placed Albee's bowl on the shelf so he could get a closer look. "This is all for you!"

"You'd butter not touch it!" Albee said. But sadly no one heard him because he's a fish.

Shivers marveled at the rest of the room. There was a giant microwave so he could make popcorn and heat up old pizza at the same time. The windowsill was decorated with pots full of daisies and sunflowers.

"We got you a flower bed," said Bob, beaming.

"Awww," said Shivers. "I'll have to get some flower pillows and a cozy flower blankie!"

Before Bob could explain what a flower bed actually was, Shivers saw something very disturbing on the counter. "AAAGH! A toaster!" he screamed.

"Don't worry," Tilda said, putting her arm around him and walking him carefully toward the device. "It has slow-rise popping action. See?"

Two pieces of bread rose up slowly and silently from the toaster, like a sleepy jack-in-the-box.

Shivers's eyes popped open in amazement. "It's a *slow*-ster! I love it! It's *sooo* me!"

And with that, he hopped through the door and out to the main deck, twirling with excitement. Once he reached the deck, he kept on twirling.

"Hey, I could spin out here forever!" he exclaimed.

"That's what it's made for! It's a song and dance deck," said Tilda.

Shivers stopped short and gasped. The black surface of the deck was shiny and smooth. It stretched out in front of him for what looked like miles.

"Somebody jump on the piano! Key of G!" Shivers opened his mouth to sing.

Bob interrupted him. "Sorry, Shivers, we haven't gotten you a piano yet. But we did get you this!" He held up a rotting fish skeleton.

"It's a fishbone xylophone!" said Tilda proudly. "You play it with a wishbone!"

Bob demonstrated, clinking out a few flat notes.

Shivers leaped back in disgust. "Albee would be horrified! You're lucky he's busy eating butter right now."

Bob shrugged and threw the fish carcass over the deck, where it landed on a beachgoer (who quickly became a home-goer).

Tilda smiled reassuringly. "I swear by all the squids in the sea, we'll get you that piano. But for now, this will have to just be a dance deck."

Shivers sighed. "I guess I can live with that."

Tilda knew just the thing to cheer him up. "You haven't seen what's in here!" she said, walking across the deck. She opened the door to an enormous closet, and Shivers could see that it was packed to the max with brand-new mops.

Shivers screamed in sheer delight. Next to singing and dancing, mopping was his favorite activity. He sprinted to the closet, leaped inside, and grabbed as many mops as he could. He hugged them all, nuzzling his face into their soft fuzzy mop heads. "You know what they say, 'Mop till you drop!'" Shivers picked up a bucket and tossed it to Tilda. "You get the water, I'll choose a mop, we'll meet back here in eight seconds!"

"No!" said Tilda and Bob at the same time.

"What? You need ten seconds?" Shivers asked.

"Shivers, you can't mop the deck today!" Bob barked.

"Why not?" Shivers was confused.

Bob's eyebrows furrowed into a stern scowl. His jawbones tightened with tension. Even his beard bristled nervously. He looked around cautiously, and then in a terrified whisper he uttered, "The Curse of Quincy Thomas the Pirate."

Shivers dropped all the mops. "The *what?* . . . of the *who?*"

Tilda mashed her lips with concern. She hated to tell Shivers about something so scary because he always got so screamy. But it had to be done. "If a pirate lets a single drop of water hit the deck on the day he gets a new ship, he'll be cursed by the ghost of Quincy Thomas the Pirate."

"Ghost?!" Shivers shrieked.

"Ghost?!" Bob bellowed, diving into the mop closet.

"Who said ghost?!" Tilda screeched, jumping in after Bob. Shivers followed close behind her and slammed the closet door.

"AAAAAAGGGGGGHH!"

SHIVERS!

The Pirate Who's Afraid of EVERYTHING

Meet Shivers, the scaredy-est pirate to ever sail the Seven Seas!

Visit www.shiversthepirate.com for:

- ☠ Amazing author videos
- ☠ Creative writing ideas
- ☠ Storytelling tips and tricks
- ☠ Writing prompts and activities

Art by Anthony Holden

HARPER

An Imprint of HarperCollinsPublishers